Point Horror

THE WITNESS

R.L. Stine

■ SCHOLASTIC

Scholastic Children's Books,
Scholastic Publications Ltd,
7-9 Pratt Street, London NW1 0AE, UK

Scholastic Inc.,
555 Broadway, New York, NY 10012-3999, USA

Scholastic Canada Ltd,
123 Newkirk Road, Richmond Hill,
Ontario, Canada L4C 3G5

Ashton Scholastic Pty Ltd,
PO Box 579, Gosford, New South Wales,
Australia

Ashton Scholastic Ltd,
Private Bag 92801, Penrose, Auckland,
New Zealand

First published in the US by Scholastic Inc., 1994
First published in the UK by Scholastic Publications Ltd, 1995

Copyright © Robert L. Stine, 1994

ISBN 0 590 55901 X

Printed by Cox and Wyman Ltd, Reading, Berks

10 9 8 7 6 5 4 3 2 1

The Witness

He stood above her on a jutting rock, hands at the waist of his jeans. His navy blue T-shirt fluttered in the wind.

He glared down at her with narrowed eyes, his black hair over his forehead. The sunlight caught the small silver ring in his ear, making it glow like a diamond.

Roxie gasped.

Why wasn't he locked up? Why did the police let him go?

How long had he been standing there? Did he hear her conversation with Ursula?

Frozen on the low rock, caught in the darkness of his shadow, she watched a strange smile form slowly on his face.

"Roxie," Lee said softly, "I saw you."

Look out for:

Nightmare Hall:
The Wish
Diane Hoh

The Yearbook
Peter Lerangis

The Forbidden Game 1:
The Hunter
L. J. Smith

Prologue

Roxie pressed her back against the wall and stared down into the darkness.

From somewhere downstairs she heard the girl cry out angrily.

Then she heard the sound of a slap.

Roxie flinched and raised her hands, as if she herself had been slapped.

Downstairs, the girl cried out again, her anger replaced by shrill fear.

The boy muttered a low curse.

Another hard slap.

The sound shot through Roxie's body like an electrical shock. She gripped the banister with a cold, damp hand. Her chest ached. She realized she'd been holding her breath the whole time.

I've got to get out of here! Roxie told herself.

But her legs were trembling too hard to walk.

She heard the girl cry out, heard ugly groans. "Let go of me!" the girl pleaded.

Roxie pressed her back harder against the wall. She saw that she was halfway down the stairs. The front door lay just beyond a short entryway.

I've got to move! Got to get out of this house!

But could she get past the living room without being seen?

What am I doing here? Roxie asked herself, listening hard. Now all she could hear were the hoarse gasps of her own breathing.

Why am I hiding in this house?

Did I really break in because of a stupid bet?

Gripping the banister, she eased herself down one step. It creaked under her weight.

She swallowed hard. Did they hear?

No.

Roxie heard a loud crash. She heard more groans. Scuffling.

Is he going to *kill* her? The terrifying thought flashed into her mind.

Am I actually going to stand here and *listen* to a murder?

Chapter 1

"Care to make a little bet?" Ursula Nordquist asked, bending to pull up her white socks.

"No way!" Roxie Nelson replied, spinning her tennis racket impatiently. "If I bet you, you won't let me win a single game." She raised a hand to shield her eyes from the bright sun. "Come on, Ursula, we only have the court for an hour."

Ursula stood up and straightened the white skirt of her tennis outfit. Her short, white-blond hair caught the sunlight. Her blue eyes flashed. She pulled the white visor over her forehead and adjusted her sunglasses. "A five-dollar bet," she insisted. "I'll play into the sun — just to make it competitive."

"What a sport," Roxie muttered, rolling her eyes. "Why can't we ever just play a relaxed, friendly game?"

"That's what I want," Ursula insisted, leading the way through the gate onto the court. "A relaxed, friendly game for five dollars."

They both laughed.

Ursula's sense of humor is her saving grace, Roxie thought. Otherwise, I'd have to kill her!

Roxie watched her friend walk to the far side of the court. Ursula moved in long, graceful strides. She always looks like some sort of Norwegian snow princess, Roxie thought. Even in this blazing heat.

Ursula had a white streak of sunscreen on the back of one of her long, perfect legs. Upon arriving at the tennis courts, she had carefully rubbed the stuff over every inch of her pale skin. "I don't burn. I stroke," Ursula joked.

Roxie had dark features, brown hair, and dark brown eyes, and her skin tanned easily. She was short, one of the shortest girls in her class at Jackson High. And her figure could only be described as boyish.

"I want to look like you," she had confessed to Ursula early in their friendship. "You're like a tall, graceful Afghan hound, and I'm a long-haired dachshund."

"Why do you have to make us dogs?" Ursula had complained.

But Roxie could see that Ursula was secretly pleased by the compliment. Ursula liked compliments.

She likes to be the prettiest, Roxie realized. She is so competitive. She likes to be the best at everything. Maybe that's why Ursula keeps me around as her best friend.

But that was unfair, Roxie knew. Despite her need to always come out on top, Ursula *was* a good friend. She was generous and understanding, a good listener, and she had always been there when Roxie needed her.

"Volley for serve," Ursula called. She adjusted her sun visor, then lowered herself into a ready stance.

Roxie's first serve went into the net.

The second attempt sailed into the net, too.

"You're getting better," Ursula teased. "Three or four more tries, and you'll clear it!"

Roxie was sweating already. The sunlight reflected off the asphalt court, making it appear to shimmer.

Ursula won the first set easily. She barely had to move, while Roxie found herself darting and lunging from one side of the court to the other.

Roxie raised her racket to serve, but Ursula held up a hand to signal time-out. She strode over to her white canvas bag and pulled out a large plastic bottle of Evian water. After taking a long drink and splashing some on her neck, Ursula returned to the court.

They started to play again. Roxie switched to her two-handed backhand, trying to get back in the game. "Hey! All right!" she cried out when she finally slammed one past Ursula.

"Where's Terry?" Ursula asked, tossing Roxie another ball. "What's he doing this summer? Hanging out at the beach?"

Roxie shook her head. "He started working today. At his father's store."

"Yuck!" Ursula made a disgusted face. "Terry's going to work at the fish store? He'll smell!"

Roxie served, then moved forward to get ready for Ursula's return. "He's just delivering. He says he won't smell too bad."

"You're going to need a new boyfriend," Ursula said, returning Roxie's serve easily. "Terry's going to smell. Every time you kiss him, you'll think you're kissing a dead halibut."

Roxie laughed.

Ursula didn't like Terry. She always complained that he was too loud and crude, too stuck on himself.

Roxie decided that maybe Ursula was a little

jealous. Roxie had a steady boyfriend and Ursula didn't. It was the one area of their lives where Roxie came out on top — for now, anyway.

"Are you getting a job this summer?" Roxie asked. She swung hard and missed the ball. It bounced against the wire fence with a loud *clang*.

"I can't get a job," Ursula replied, twirling her racket. "I might break a nail."

They both laughed.

"Seriously, I'm working a couple of mornings a week at school," Ursula confided, pulling up her white socks again. "In the office."

"Doing what?" Roxie asked, groaning as she sent a serve skimming over the net.

"They're transferring all the files to the computer," Ursula replied, returning the serve easily. "I'm helping keyboard the stuff. It's real boring, but it's six bucks an hour."

"Maybe I'll see you there," Roxie said, using her two-handed backhand to return the ball.

"Out!" Ursula cried.

I *hate* the way she calls out, Roxie decided. Like it's such a thrill for her.

"I'm taking a course in summer school," Roxie said.

"What course?" Ursula asked, picking up a ball, preparing to serve.

Roxie rolled her eyes. "French, of course. I'm so retarded in French. I really need the extra classes."

A car horn honked on the street. Roxie turned to see a bunch of kids she knew jammed into a blue minivan. She waved. The driver honked again.

They were heading to the beach. Wiping the sweat off her forehead with the sleeve of her T-shirt, Roxie suddenly wished she was joining them.

Rocky Shores was a pretty boring, isolated place in the winter, she thought. But in the summer, living in a beach town was the best! You didn't have to go away to spend the summer swimming and sunning. You just had to drive down Main Street till you came to the beach.

Sure, Treasure Beach wasn't the most beautiful beach in the world. It had a lot more rocks and pebbles than sand. That's why the town was called Rocky Shores.

And it was on the sound, not on the ocean. Which meant the waves weren't good for surfing.

But it was a perfect meeting place for all the

kids from Jackson High. A perfect place to meet kids from other towns, kids staying in the rented cottages and small tourist inns and motels that dotted Dune Road. A perfect place to hang out from morning till night if you didn't have a summer job.

At night, the beach became a romantic meeting place. Boom boxes blared. Kids gathered on blankets or around small fires to laugh and to party.

Roxie loved Rocky Shores in the summer. It made up for all the gray, cold winter days when she wished she lived in a bigger town, somewhere far away from the freezing winds that blew in off the water.

"Maybe we should go to the beach," she suggested, mopping her forehead with her sleeve again.

"No way!" Ursula insisted. "The water is still too cold. It's only June. I never go in until the end of July."

Roxie laughed. "What if we go to the beach and I bet you five dollars I can get into the water and swim before you do?" she asked slyly.

"No way," Ursula replied, shaking her head. "I'd lose that bet. And I never make a bet that I'm going to lose."

That's for sure! Roxie thought with some bitterness.

Ursula lobbed a high return over the net. Roxie started back, lost it in the bright sky for a moment, back, back. "Ow!" She collided with the wire fence. Pain shot up her arm. The racket flew from her hand and clattered across the asphalt.

"Are you okay?" Ursula called.

Before Roxie could reply, she heard a loud cry behind her on the street.

She spun around and peered through the fence.

A red-haired girl came running toward the tennis courts. "Roxie! Hey — Roxie! Help me!"

Roxie recognized her friend Shawna Cohn. She started to call out a greeting — but choked on the words as Shawna came into view.

And Roxie saw that Shawna's clothes were covered in bright red blood.

"Roxie — help me!" Shawna cried.

Chapter 2

Both girls dropped their tennis rackets and hurried to help their friend. "Shawna — what happened?" Roxie cried, running through the gate.

"It's Lee!" Shawna exclaimed. "He — he — "

"He *cut* you?" Ursula cried shrilly.

Roxie put a comforting arm around Shawna's trembling shoulders. "*What* did Lee do?"

"Nothing," Shawna replied, lowering her gaze to her bloodstained shorts and midriff shirt. "He — broke up with me." She pushed back her red hair with one hand.

"But you're *bleeding*!" Roxie cried.

"I — I was so stupid," Shawna stammered. "I tried to hit him and I cut my hand on the side of his boat." She held out her hand, revealing a one-inch cut at the wrist, still oozing bright red blood.

"We've got to stop the bleeding," Ursula said, eyeing the cut with a frown. Her expression turned suspicious. "Are you sure Lee didn't hurt you? I've heard he has a real temper."

Shawna rolled her eyes. "Tell me about it," she muttered. She raised the bleeding wrist to examine it. "Ow. I can't believe I was such a jerk. I did it to myself. He moved out of the way, and my arm hit a blade on the outboard motor."

"Ow!" Roxie cried sympathetically. "Didn't he see you were bleeding? Didn't he offer to help?"

"I didn't want him to," Shawna replied bitterly. "I was so upset and angry. I just turned and ran off the dock. I was running home. Then I saw you two, and — "

"Maybe we should get you to the emergency room. Ursula has her car here," Roxie said, glancing at Ursula's white Chrysler convertible in the parking lot.

"You have to promise not to bleed in the car," Ursula called from the tennis court. "It's got white seats."

"You're a real pal," Shawna murmured sarcastically.

Ursula searched through her white canvas bag and pulled out a red bandanna. "Here. We can wrap your wrist in this."

A few seconds later, they had the wrist tightly wrapped. Roxie gathered up the tennis rackets. Then they piled into Ursula's car and headed to North Shore General Hospital, in the next town.

Shawna sat in the front of the convertible beside Ursula, staring down at the red bandanna, shaking her head unhappily. Roxie sat in the center of the backseat, the wind blowing her dark hair behind her like a pennant.

Shawna was saying something, something about Lee, Roxie thought. She struggled to hear her over the roar of the wind. But the only words Roxie caught were: "I can't believe he broke up with me."

Roxie found herself thinking about Lee Blume. She pictured his tanned face, his slim, athletic-looking body, his dark eyes under his straight black hair. Soulful eyes, she thought.

He had a tiny silver ring in one ear. And a mysterious white scar on his chin. He wore a blue-and-silver Sharks cap. He almost never took it off.

He spoke very softly. Roxie couldn't remember ever hearing him shout. She couldn't remember seeing him smile, either.

Lee was really great-looking, Roxie thought, in a sullen, moody kind of way.

She closed her eyes against the bright sunlight, letting the wind whip through her hair as the convertible sped past the rocky dunes. She pictured herself walking on the beach with Lee.

Roxie admitted to herself that she had been attracted to him from the day he started at Jackson High the past fall. She didn't really know why. Maybe it was his dark good looks. Maybe it was his quiet manner, his soft voice, his thoughtful eyes.

Maybe it was just because Lee was new, not one of the boys from Rocky Shores that Roxie had known since the age of five.

Roxie remembered walking up to Lee at his locker a few days after he had started school. She offered to show him around Rocky Shores. It had taken all of her nerve to come on to him like that. Roxie had always been more than a little shy with boys.

Lee had turned his dark eyes on her. "Hey, thanks," he had replied without smiling. "I'll call you sometime."

But he never did.

The next thing Roxie knew, he was going out with Shawna.

And by October, Roxie had started seeing Terry.

Terry, she realized, was sort of the opposite of Lee. He was big and funny and loud. No mystery at all to Terry. What you saw was what you got.

Even though Roxie was really fond of Terry, she still found herself thinking about Lee from time to time. And sometimes when she saw Shawna and Lee together, Roxie had to fight back the feelings of envy that swept over her.

Now, Shawna's angry voice from the front seat of the speeding convertible interrupted Roxie's thoughts. "Everyone thinks he's so quiet," Shawna was saying. "They haven't seen his temper tantrums the way I have."

I'd *like* to see his temper tantrums, Roxie thought wistfully. I'd really like to get to know Lee Blume.

The tall redbrick hospital building loomed into view. Ursula pulled the car up the drive to the emergency room entrance. As the car squealed to a stop, Roxie shook away her thoughts about Lee, and hurried to help her friend.

*   *   *

Two days later, Roxie ran into Lee.

She and Ursula were taking a late-afternoon walk on the beach. Carrying their sandals, they strolled side by side, close to the shore, their bare feet sliding over the smooth pebbles, the cold water lapping at their ankles.

Ursula had a white shirt tied at her waist over her pale blue bikini. Roxie wore a sleeveless white T-shirt over white denim cutoffs.

Small puffs of white cloud dotted the late afternoon sky. The sun hovered low over the dark rock cliffs behind them.

"How's Shawna doing?" Ursula asked.

"Fine," Roxie replied, bending to pick up a smooth white pebble. "I talked to her this morning. Guess who she's going out with Saturday night? Barry Walker."

Ursula laughed. Her cold blue eyes sparkled. "Busy girl," she said dryly. "Guess she's gotten over Lee."

And just as she said the name, both girls raised their eyes to the small dock at the end of the swimming area — and saw Lee staring at them.

"Hey — hi!" Ursula called, raising her hand above her head and waving to him.

Lee didn't smile. Roxie watched him adjust

the Sharks cap over his dark hair as the two girls approached the dock.

Lee's bright yellow cigarette boat bobbed in the water beside the dock. Often when Roxie would come to the beach, she would see Lee scooting around in the sleek little boat. Watching from shore, she would see the yellow boat slapping over the low waves, hear the soft roar of its motor as Lee raced back and forth out in the open waters.

It looks like fun, Roxie had always thought longingly.

Terry didn't like the beach. He had red hair and very fair skin and was always afraid of getting sunburned.

"How's it going?" Lee asked softly as Roxie and Ursula stepped out onto the dock. The old boards gave under their feet. The entire dock bobbed in the water. Roxie raised both arms to catch her balance.

"Nice day," Ursula said, tossing back her white-blond hair as she flashed him a warm smile.

"Yeah. Water's a little choppy," Lee replied, motioning out to the sparkling, low waves.

Roxie struggled to think of something to say. Ursula had stepped in front of her and was acting as if Roxie wasn't even there.

Typical! Roxie thought bitterly.

"I like your boat," Ursula told him. "It's so shiny. Is it . . . plastic?"

He adjusted the Sharks cap. "No. Fiberglas."

"Is it yours?" Ursula asked, her eyes on the bobbing boat.

Lee nodded. "My dad gave it to me. For my birthday."

"That's great!" Roxie exclaimed, desperate to join the conversation.

"Want a ride?" Lee offered, his eyes trained on Ursula.

"Now?" Ursula asked.

"Yeah. Sure. I was just going to take her out," Lee replied. He reached for the rope and pulled the boat closer to the dock.

Roxie held back. Lee hadn't even looked at her. He hadn't been able to take his eyes off Ursula in her pale blue bikini. Was he inviting only Ursula?

"There's room for you, too," Lee told Roxie, as if reading her mind.

"Thanks," she replied awkwardly. She could feel her face growing hot.

Dark shadows suddenly flitted over the narrow dock, startling Roxie. She started to duck before she realized they were caused by low-flying sea gulls heading to the shore.

When she glanced back up, she saw Lee staring at her.

He thinks I'm a total jerk! she told herself. I should just throw myself off the dock and drown.

"Come on," Lee urged quietly. "A short ride."

He lowered himself easily into the boat. He moves so gracefully, Roxie thought. The slender yellow boat bobbed and swayed under his weight.

Standing, he helped the two girls down. Ursula took the middle seat. Her blue eyes flashed excitedly. Roxie found herself in back. The yellow seat was wet. The cold water soaked through her cutoffs.

Their weight made the boat rest low in the water. The motor started up easily. The roar drowned out all other sounds — the wash of the waves, the shrill call of the gulls, the voices of the late afternoon sunbathers on the beach.

With a hard jolt that almost threw Roxie off the seat, the boat roared away from the dock. Waves of water tossed up on both sides. The little boat slapped and leaped over the on-rushing waves.

"This is great!" Roxie shouted, holding on tightly to the sides. The cold spray felt won-

derful on her face. The cool rush of wind blew
her hair wildly behind her.

Ursula grinned back at her and flashed her
a thumbs-up.

Roxie turned back to see the beach moving
farther and farther away. The red sun had
nearly lowered itself to the rock cliffs. Sea gulls
swerved and dipped low to the shore.

It's so beautiful, Roxie thought as they
bounced over the choppy waves, heading out
to open waters. Red sunlight reflected in the
water made the waves sparkle like bright ru-
bies. She pushed tangles of hair off her forehead to let the cool spray hit her face.

Lee held his cap on with one hand, steering
the boat with the other. Two sailboats shimmered into view, far to the right. The beach
appeared miles away now.

Roxie turned her gaze to Lee. He stared
straight ahead, his dark eyes narrowed as he
guided the boat. Roxie found herself gaping at
his tanned arms. She had never realized how
muscular he was. He had always seemed slender and kind of slight to her. He must work
out, she realized.

She was still staring at his arms when the
roar stopped.

Roxie's mouth dropped open, startled by the sudden silence.

She could hear the rush of water now, waves slapping under and around the boat.

It took her a moment to realize the engine had stopped.

Ursula let out a nervous laugh. "What's up, Lee?" she called.

Lee ignored her question. He fiddled with the controls.

When he turned back to them, his features were tight with worry. "It . . . it conked out," he said in a trembling voice. "It's totally dead. We're drifting out to open sea!"

Chapter 3

A tall wave slapped the side of the boat, jolting them sideways. The boat bobbed helplessly in the current.

Roxie turned her gaze to the beach. It seemed a million miles away. The sun had started to sink behind the jutting, dark cliffs. The shore was cloaked in shadow.

"Can't you get it started again?" Ursula demanded, gripping the sides of the boat with her hands as if trying to steady it.

"It's totally dead," Lee repeated.

"Well, maybe someone can see us," Roxie suggested, her eyes darting around the sound. The two sailboats had disappeared from view. The sun dipped and the water darkened, as if a dark blanket was being pulled over it.

"Or hear us!" Roxie added. She tossed her

head and started to shout: "Help! Help! Somebody!"

The wind seemed to blow her words back into her face.

She stopped to take a breath — and realized that Lee was laughing.

"Gotcha!" he declared, his dark eyes narrowed gleefully.

Roxie realized it was the first time she had ever heard Lee laugh. Such cruel laughter, she thought.

"You mean — ?" Roxie started. She could feel her face growing hot and knew she was blushing. She had made a total fool of herself.

And Lee was enjoying every moment of it.

Ursula playfully pounded Lee's back with both fists. "You jerk!" she cried, laughing. "Like to play mean tricks?"

"Yeah," Lee replied, his grin fading, his dark eyes suddenly serious. "I'm mean. I'm a real mean dude."

A strong wave tossed the boat back. Lee turned to the controls and started up the motor. He turned the boat toward shore.

What a dumb joke, Roxie thought, frowning.

This is one boat ride I'd like to forget.

But a few days later, when things turned

really ugly and frightening, she remembered Lee's narrowed eyes, and his words: "I'm mean. I'm a real mean dude."

The next morning after her French class, Roxie met Ursula in the school office. Roxie leaned against the long counter and greeted her friend, seated in front of a computer on the other side.

Ursula had tied her hair back in a blue ribbon, which perfectly matched the color of her eyes. She glanced up from her computer keyboard and smiled as Roxie leaned over the counter.

"What's up?" Ursula asked.

Roxie glanced around the outer office. Ursula was the only one working. She could see the light on in the principal's office in back, and heard women's voices behind the closed door.

"They're just having lunch," Ursula told her. "There are three of us keyboarding the files." She sighed. "At least it's cloudy today. I don't feel so bad about not being at the beach. How's French?"

It was Roxie's turn to sigh. "The same."

She lowered her gaze to the desk and her eyes caught the name on the open file. "Lee?" she uttered. "You have Lee Blume's file?"

Ursula nodded. "Yeah. Just . . . uh . . . checking out his address. He lives on Seabreeze. A few blocks from the pine woods."

Roxie thought about their ride in Lee's yellow cigarette boat. It had been so much fun until he pulled that stupid joke on them. She still felt embarrassed about shouting for help as loudly as she could.

"Why do you need his address?" she asked Ursula. "Thinking of dropping by?"

"Maybe he'd like to buy some Girl Scout cookies," Ursula said playfully.

"You're not a Girl Scout," Roxie reminded her.

"So?"

They both laughed.

Ursula cut her laugh off first. "You like him, too, don't you, Roxie!" It was said as an accusation. Ursula stared hard at Roxie until Roxie could feel her face growing hot.

"He's okay," Roxie said. She tried to sound nonchalant, but she could feel her face grow even hotter.

"What would Terry say?" Ursula demanded in a teasing singsong.

"Terry and I went to the movies last night," Roxie said, changing the subject.

"And did you tell him we were stranded out on Lee's boat?" Ursula teased.

Roxie made a disgusted face. "Actually, I didn't mention it."

"That's because you're hot for Lee's bod," Ursula commented, tapping her dark red fingernails on Lee's file.

"Don't be crude," Roxie scolded.

"I'm lewd and crude," Ursula boasted. Lewd and crude was one of her favorite phrases. She described just about everyone and everything as lewd and crude. "What if I tell Terry that you're hot for Lee's bod?"

"Not funny, Ursula," Roxie replied seriously.

"But what if I do?" Ursula teased.

"If you do, I'll tell everyone you're not a natural blond!" Roxie exclaimed.

Ursula gasped. "But I *am*!"

Roxie laughed. "I know you are. But who are they going to believe? Everyone will believe me — not you."

Ursula's eyes burned into Roxie's. "Sometimes you surprise me, Roxie," she said thoughtfully.

"Is that supposed to be a compliment?" Roxie shot back.

Ursula shifted in her desk chair. They could hear laughter in the inner office. Outside the window, the sky darkened, threatening a storm.

"Bet I could get a date with Lee before you," Ursula said in a low voice just above a whisper. She stared up at Roxie, challenging her.

Roxie sighed. "Not another bet," she murmured, rolling her brown eyes.

Secretly, Roxie thought: Maybe this is one bet I could win against Ursula.

And then she thought: It might be fun to try.

And then she thought: Am I totally losing it? I've *never* won a bet against Ursula. Never!

"Let's make this a good one," Ursula said, a devilish smile making her blue eyes crinkle at the corners. "How about fifty dollars?"

"Whoa!" Roxie cried. "Are you kidding? No way!"

"Tell you what," Ursula continued excitedly. "If you go out with Lee before me, I'll pay the fifty bucks — and I'll help tutor you in French for the rest of the summer."

Roxie laughed. "Well . . . *that's* kind of tempting." But her smile quickly faded. "Wait a minute. Whoa. What am I saying?"

Ursula tapped her long fingernails on the file beside her. "What's wrong?"

"It could be the shortest bet in the history of the world," Roxie replied, shaking her head. "You call Lee up. You ask him out. He says yes. End of bet. And I'm out fifty bucks."

Ursula grinned. "That's about the way I see it."

"Well, it isn't a fair bet!" Roxie declared heatedly. "You're a lot less shy than I am. I can't just call him and ask him out. I'm not like that."

"Boo-hoo," Ursula replied sarcastically. "Let me get out my hanky and we'll all have a good cry."

Roxie ignored her friend's teasing. She was thinking hard. She thought she had a better idea. An idea to make the bet more fair. And more interesting.

"Let's make the bet a little harder," she suggested.

Ursula's eyes lit up. "Harder? You mean I have to be gagged and blindfolded and have one hand tied behind my back? And I can speak only Norwegian?"

Roxie shook her head impatiently. "Let's say that to win the bet, you have to go out with Lee — and you have to get him to give you his Sharks cap."

"Huh?" Ursula climbed to her feet. She

pressed her hands against her waist. "We have to *what*?"

"You have to come to school the next morning wearing Lee's Sharks cap," Roxie repeated.

Ursula didn't have to think about it long. "I like it," she said, grinning. "It's a bet. Shake." She reached across the counter and shook Roxie's hand.

"And what about Terry?" Ursula demanded.

Roxie shrugged. "What's one date? What he doesn't know won't hurt him."

"Right," Ursula agreed. "Well, good luck."

"Huh?" Roxie cried in surprise. "You're actually wishing me good luck?"

"Yeah," Ursula replied, grinning. "Good luck raising the fifty bucks. You'll need it to pay me by next week at the latest!"

Roxie laughed.

It seemed like a simple bet. A fun bet between best friends.

Who would ever believe it would lead Roxie to a horrifying murder?

Chapter 4

"Put me down! I mean it, Terry!"

Terry let out a fiendish laugh.

Roxie kicked her legs hard, trying to squirm free. But Terry was too strong for her. He carried her over the pebbly beach to the shore. Then he started swinging her over the edge of the water, threatening to toss her in.

"Put me down!" Roxie squealed, laughing.

Instead, Terry began to run, raising his knees high. Into the water. "Whoa!" he cried out as he slipped on the smooth, round rocks under his feet.

About ten feet out, the rocks gave way to soft sand. Terry kept running until the low waves were at his waist.

"Put me down, Terry! I mean it!" Roxie shrieked.

"Okay!" With a devilish grin, he let go of her.

Roxie hit the water hard. Terry dived under.

They both came up, sputtering and laughing.

"It's *freezing*!" Roxie cried. She ducked under again, came up quickly, and spit a stream of water into his face.

"Hey!" Terry protested and splashed waves of water over her with both hands.

"Okay! I give! I give!" Roxie cried, raising her hands in surrender. She swung an arm around his broad shoulder and let him carry them further out.

There are some advantages to being short and scrawny, she told herself.

The bright sun high overhead made the water sparkle like gold. The breeze was soft and cool. Behind them, the beach was crowded with sunbathers. Several teenagers had started a loud, energetic volleyball game. Near the dock, some kids were trying to windsurf, even though the breeze was so light.

Her arm slid off Terry and she swam beside him, taking long strokes to keep up. His swimming always made her laugh. He was so big and uncoordinated.

"What's so funny?" he demanded, rolling onto his back to face her. "I swim like a fish."

"More like a beached whale!" Roxie exclaimed.

He reached out and playfully ducked her head under the water. They swam a short while longer, then wrestled and splashed their way back to the beach.

Grabbing a towel, Roxie dropped onto the red-and-white blanket they had spread on the beach near the dock. She ran the towel over her brown hair, then draped it over her shoulders.

Terry stood beside her, dripping water. He pushed back his red, curly hair as he studied the volleyball game down the beach.

"Nice day, huh?" Roxie asked, beaming up at him. She felt very happy. Terry had been moody lately, probably because he had to spend the summer working at his father's fish store. And he really didn't like the beach.

But today they were having such a good time. The first really good day since school had let out two weeks before.

"Want to get in the game?" Terry asked, swatting a fly on his freckled shoulder.

"Well . . ." Roxie hesitated. She didn't like

volleyball. When she played up close, she was too short to hit the ball over the net.

"Come on. Let's play," Terry urged, reaching down to tug her to her feet.

She allowed him to pull her up — then gasped. "Hey — wait!" She pulled her hand free and stared hard at the dock.

Yes! The tall, beautiful blond in the white bikini was Ursula. She was standing at the end of the dock — talking to Lee.

I can't let her win the bet!

The thought flashed through Roxie's mind. And before she even realized it, she had left Terry behind and was running as fast as she could over the pebbly beach to the dock.

"Hi, guys! Hi!" Roxie shouted, her feet slapping the damp wooden boards.

Ursula and Lee turned toward her, startled expressions on their faces. "Roxie!" Ursula cried without enthusiasm. "What's up?"

"Hi!" Roxie cried breathlessly, grinning at Lee. "Nice day, huh?"

Lee nodded. He wore a faded blue muscle shirt and baggy denim cutoffs. His dark hair tumbled out from beneath his Sharks cap.

He looks awesome, Roxie thought. So tanned and handsome. I can't let Ursula win this one. I really can't.

But do I stand a chance? He barely says a word to me.

The yellow cigarette boat bobbed beside the dock. "Lee and I were just going to take her out," Ursula commented, seeing Roxie's eyes on the boat. She turned to Lee. "No jokes this time, right?"

"Maybe," he replied, his dark eyes lighting up as he gazed back at Ursula.

Ursula flashed Roxie a knowing smile. A victory smile, Roxie thought bitterly. As if Ursula was already claiming that she had won.

For a brief moment, Roxie pictured herself pushing her friend off the dock, then climbing into the boat with Lee.

Terry's calls interrupted her fantasy. "Hey — what's up?"

They all turned to see him lumbering over the dock, pulling up his baggy red-and-blue swim trunks as he ran. "Do you know Terry?" Ursula asked Lee. "Roxie's boyfriend?"

Roxie clenched her teeth hard. Ursula added that deliberately, she knew. She told Lee that Terry was my boyfriend just to make sure I don't stand a chance with our bet.

Terry stepped up beside Roxie and put his arm around her shoulders. "Hi, guys," he said cheerily.

Terry acts like he owns me, Roxie thought bitterly. Like I'm his puppy dog or something. She stepped sideways to get out from under his heavy arm.

The four of them talked for a short while, mostly about what they were doing that summer. Roxie kept smiling at Lee. But he didn't seem to notice her at all. Beneath his Sharks cap, his dark eyes stayed on Ursula.

"Lee and I were going for a ride," Ursula said, motioning to the bobbing yellow boat. Her lips formed a pout. "But there isn't room for four."

"Sorry." Lee shrugged. He seemed eager to get into the boat.

It's all over, Roxie thought glumly. *I've lost already.*

"Maybe we could all do something tonight," she suggested desperately. "You know. A picnic on the beach or something."

Ursula had a strange, tight grin on her face. She knew what was on Roxie's mind.

Lee shook his head, frowning. "Can't," he said softly. "I have to go to a stupid charity thing at the club with my parents tonight."

"Too bad," Roxie murmured, trying not to appear as disappointed as she felt. "How about tomorrow night?" she blurted out.

"I don't know," Lee replied, gazing at Ursula. "I'm not too good at planning ahead."

Roxie felt embarrassed. She knew she was being too eager, too obvious.

She could feel Terry's eyes on her. She stepped back as Lee lowered himself into the boat, then helped Ursula down. Roxie saw his hands remain on Ursula's slender, pale shoulders a little longer than they needed to.

No, Roxie thought angrily. *No. No. No!*
She can't win that easily!
I won't let her! I really won't!

Ursula smiled up at Roxie and waved.

Roxie turned and began making her way back to the blanket, thinking furiously.

Terry hurried to catch up to her, his bare feet slapping the wooden planks. "What was *that* about?" he called.

Roxie heard Lee's boat start up with a roar. She kept walking fast without turning back.

Terry caught up with her. "Why did you rush over to them like that?" he demanded suspiciously. "You took off like a shot!"

"I — I just wanted to say hi to Ursula," Roxie told him.

"But you didn't even *look* at Ursula," Terry replied, his eyes searching her face.

"Oh. Right." She wasn't really listening to Terry.

Roxie suddenly had an idea.

It popped into her mind. An idea that would win the bet for her.

"What are you smiling about?" Terry demanded as they dropped back onto the blanket.

"Just smiling," Roxie replied, lost in her scheming thoughts.

It was a sneaky trick. A dangerous trick. Really unfair and underhanded.

She knew she had to do it.

Chapter 5

Roxie pulled her car to the curb and cut the lights. She waited for her eyes to adjust to the darkness.

There aren't any streetlights on Seabreeze, she realized.

She took a deep breath and climbed out of the car. Glancing up, she saw that there wasn't even any moonlight to light her way. Low, dark clouds blanketed the sky.

The clouds had rolled in off the sound in the late afternoon. Just before dinnertime, it had rained for about twenty minutes. Then the rain stopped abruptly, leaving the air hot and sticky.

Roxie's sneakers crunched on the gravelly pavement as she gazed up at the house. It was completely dark. Not even a porch light. The house hovered heavily at the top of the sloping front lawn, like a big creature waiting for its prey.

Roxie stopped at the bottom of the gravel driveway and leaned against the mailbox on its pole, struggling to read the number.

I don't want to break into the wrong house, she thought, wishing her heart wasn't thudding so hard in her chest.

The number on the box was 133. That was Lee's number. Roxie had memorized it from the file Ursula had on her desk in the office at school.

Well, here I am, she thought wistfully.

She gazed up at the large, dark-shingled house again.

Here I am, about to break into Lee's house.

At least he told the truth about having to go out with his parents tonight. The dark windows showed there was no one home.

Roxie's plan was simple. She was going to enter Lee's house, go up to his room, find the Shark's cap, and take it.

The cap *had* to be there, she knew. Lee's parents would never let him wear it to a charity function at the club.

The next day, Roxie planned to wear the

Sharks cap to summer school and parade around in it in front of Ursula. She planned to tell Ursula that she met Lee after the charity thing, that she went back to his room with him — and he gave her the cap.

As she slowly made her way up the gravel driveway, Roxie gripped the automatic flash camera she had strapped around her neck. I'll take a few pictures of Lee's room, she had decided.

The idea had made her laugh out loud. She pictured the jealous look on Ursula's face when Roxie showed her the photos — and proved to Ursula that she had been in Lee's room!

She'll be green! Green! Roxie thought gleefully.

And for once, *I'll* be the winner. I'll win the bet. I'll win the fifty dollars. And Ursula will have to tutor me in French for the rest of the summer.

Sure, it's a cheat, Roxie knew. Sure, it's unfair.

But so what?

Is it fair that Ursula is so tall and beautiful? Is it fair that she has that perfect blond hair and those amazing blue eyes?

No. Not fair.

She swallowed hard, gazing up at the house, black against the blue-black sky. Her sneakers crunched quietly over the gravel driveway. As she passed underneath it, an old sycamore tree shivered down cold drops of water on her head and shoulders.

Roxie stopped at the end of the front walk. A small concrete stoop led to the wooden front door.

I know Ursula won't believe me, Roxie thought, staring hard at the closed door. I know she'll go running to Lee and ask if my story is true.

And of course Lee will deny it.

And then I'll tell Ursula he's lying. I'll say, "Ursula, Lee won't admit he was with me and gave me his cap, because he wants to go out with you. But pictures don't lie. How would I get pictures of his room unless I was there with him?"

And then Ursula will have to believe me.

And she'll have to admit that I finally won a bet.

Roxie had it all worked out. She'd been thinking about nothing else all afternoon and evening.

Did she feel bad about cheating against Ursula?

No, she realized. Not at all.

Ursula was the most competitive person in the world. Ursula would do *anything* to win. So why shouldn't Roxie?

She felt a shiver down her back as she climbed the three steps onto the front stoop. A long-handled wooden push broom leaned against the doorframe. Roxie nearly knocked it over as she reached for the door handle with a trembling hand.

She caught the broom as it toppled back, and nearly fell off the stoop with it.

Calm down! she scolded herself, setting the broom back in place. *There's no one around. This is going to be easy.*

Easy?

Was she really breaking into someone's house?

She turned the doorknob and pushed.

The front door was locked.

She tried it again. No. Locked.

The wind picked up. Cold drops of water rained down on her from the shuddering trees.

Car headlights rolled over the lawn, making the wet grass glisten.

Roxie leaped off the stoop and ducked behind a low evergreen shrub. The car passed by slowly, rock music blaring out of its open windows.

Roxie waited behind the shrub until the music faded away. Then she stood up, her knees trembling.

"Let's get this over with," she muttered to herself, "before I have a heart attack."

Maybe the back door isn't locked, she thought.

She jogged to the driveway, then headed toward the back of the house. The garage door was open, revealing only blackness inside.

Roxie imagined a snarling black dog leaping out of the garage, lunging at her, knocking her down, its drooling jaws clamping around her throat.

I have too much imagination, she told herself. Too much imagination is not helpful when you are about to break into a dark house.

She stopped when a side door suddenly appeared out of the blue shadows. She stepped closer.

A concrete block led up to a torn screen

door, which enclosed a wooden door behind it.

The wind fluttered the trees again. They all whispered at once, as if telling her to go away. The low sky grew even blacker.

Roxie stepped onto the concrete block and pulled open the screen door. It creaked loudly as it opened.

Roxie's hand trembled as she reached for the doorknob. She realized she was holding her breath. She let it all out in a long *whoosh*.

The doorknob turned. She pushed the door in easily.

Darkness greeted her on the other side.

Roxie stepped quickly into it and pushed the door shut behind her.

I'm in, she thought, her heart racing. I'm in the house.

She stared hard into the blackness, struggling to see where she was.

I'm in Lee's house.

I'm really doing this.

She reached out — and swallowed hard as her hand touched something soft and stringy. And damp.

Hair. Someone's hair.

"Uhhhh!" A low moan escaped Roxie's

throat. Her hand grasped the hair. Long hair. Girl's hair.

Someone is here in the darkness with me, Roxie realized, pulling her hand back in terror.

Someone is here. Someone cold and dead.

Chapter 6

Roxie's hand slapped the wall. She fumbled for a lightswitch.

She knew she shouldn't turn on any lights.

But she had no choice now. She had felt the cold, slimy hair. There was a body here beside her, still and silent.

"Uhhhhh." Another low moan escaped her throat. A sound she had never made before.

Her hand rubbed over a lightswitch. She bumped it on.

Gray light flickered over the narrow entry-way. She found herself in some sort of back pantry.

Roxie turned to the body — and gasped.

The damp, stringy hair hung from a kitchen mop.

She had grabbed the mop head in the darkness.

With a loud sigh of relief, she quickly clicked off the light. A narrow hallway led toward the front of the house. Roxie followed it, walking blindly, trailing one hand along the wall to steady herself.

The camera bobbing at her chest suddenly felt heavy. She shuddered again, thinking about the gray, stringy mop.

Her sneakers scraped on the bare wood floor. She found herself at the front stairs. Resting her hand on the banister, she took a deep breath.

"Why didn't I bring a flashlight?" she whispered to herself.

All good burglars carry flashlights, don't they?

Roxie, you're just not a pro!

She made her way onto the bottom step and peered up the stairs. A skylight at the top allowed a shaft of pale gray light to filter down. The steps were steep, Roxie saw. And narrow.

Lee's room has got to be upstairs, she told herself.

She hesitated. Her knees felt weak. She could feel the blood pulsing at her temples.

"Up!" she urged herself. She grabbed the

banister tightly in one hand and pulled herself up the steep, creaking stairs.

The camera banged into the banister, startling her. She grabbed it with her free hand, and climbed the rest of the way to the top.

This is going to be worth it, Roxie assured herself, stopping to catch her breath. I can't wait to see the look on Ursula's face when I show her the photos of Lee's bedroom!

It was hot and stuffy on the second floor, despite the coolness of the evening. The house shifted and creaked. Roxie heard every sound.

Taking a deep breath, she stepped out of the gray light from the skylight and started down the dark hall. She stopped at the first doorway and peered inside.

In the dim light from a window against the back wall, Roxie could make out a bed and dresser.

Yes. This is Lee's room.

She stepped inside and gazed at the window.

His room is at the back, she realized. So if I turn on a light, it won't be seen from the street.

Feeling a little relieved, she clicked on the ceiling light.

The room came into bright focus. An old-fashioned-looking red-and-blue quilt on the bed. Posters of basketball stars tacked on one wall, competing with two large posters of heavy metal rock groups on the adjoining wall.

Roxie's eyes darted over a cluttered bookshelf filled with magazines and books. A model of a yellow cigarette boat, much like Lee's, stood on the cluttered dressertop.

A yellow Walkman was tossed on the bed along with several cassettes. The far corner contained a pile of dirty clothes, mostly T-shirts and jeans cutoffs.

Where is the cap? she wondered. Where did he toss the Sharks cap?

Her eyes darted frantically around the small, cluttered bedroom. "Where is the cap?"

She moved to the bookshelf and searched it shelf by shelf. No Sharks cap. She bent down and shuffled through the pile of dirty clothes in the corner. No cap.

The camera bumped the floor, reminding her that she had brought it. Roxie climbed to her feet. Then she raised the camera to her eye and clicked it on. She waited for the flash indicator to turn green. Then, forcing her hand to stop shaking, she took four or five flash photos of the room.

That part of the mission accomplished, she

closed up the camera. Then she returned to her search for the cap.

Under the bed. No.

Under his pillow. No.

She pulled open the closet door. Jeans and sweatshirts and T-shirts all jammed into narrow shelves.

And on the top shelf?

Roxie reached up with both hands and pulled down the cap.

Yes!

Her heart pounded as she turned it around to look at it.

ATLANTA FALCONS. Those were the words in silver against the front of the cap.

"Arrrgh!" Roxie let out a frustrated cry. The wrong cap.

She tossed it back onto the top shelf. It took three tries to get it to stay.

When she closed the closet door, she was breathing hard.

Where can it be? Where?

She searched the desktop, then the desk drawers.

Where is it?

She was sure Lee wouldn't have taken it to the country club.

It's got to be here somewhere, she told herself.

She backed up to the doorway. Maybe I can see it better if I get a different view, she thought.

Her eyes slowly swept the room. It's not on the bed. Not under the bed. Not in the closet. Not on the shelves. Not —

"Oh!"

She let out a startled cry at the sound.

A sound she recognized at once. The sound of the front door opening downstairs.

Her heart felt as if it had leaped to her mouth. She couldn't swallow. Couldn't breathe. Couldn't move.

Frozen in the doorway to Lee's room, Roxie heard voices downstairs.

And realized she was caught.

Chapter 7

In her panic, Roxie remembered to reach up and click off the bedroom light.

Then she stood with both hands pressed against the doorframe, holding herself up, fighting back the waves of cold terror that swept over her.

She listened.

A boy's voice downstairs.

Lee?

Why was he home so early?

Roxie gasped as she heard a girl's angry shout. Shrill and high-pitched. She didn't recognize the voice.

I've got to get out of here, Roxie told herself. I've got to *move*!

Could she make it down the stairs and out the front door without being seen?

She took a step into the dark, narrow hallway and listened hard. Where were they? Were they in the front of the house? In the living room? Could they see her from there?

Roxie took another step. The floorboards creaked under her sneaker.

She stopped.

They'll hear me!

She could hear the boy speaking rapidly, angrily. Now she wasn't sure if it was Lee or not. He was speaking too softly to tell.

The boy spoke sharply, just above a whisper. Then Roxie heard a short reply from the girl. She couldn't make out the words. But she could tell they were having an argument. A very tense argument.

Step by careful step, Roxie made her way to the top of the stairs. Pressing her back against the wall of the stairwell, she peered down.

Total darkness downstairs.

Why hadn't they turned on a light? Why were they arguing in the dark?

The front door stood open, just a few feet from the bottom of the stairs.

All I have to do, Roxie thought, is run down the stairs and out the door — and I'll be free!

"Let *go* of me!" the girl shrieked.

Roxie heard scuffling. Angry curses.

"Let go! I mean it!" the girl cried.

Roxie was halfway down the stairs now. She leaned hard against the banister, trying to step lightly, trying to keep the wooden stairs from creaking.

"Ow!" The girl cried out after a loud slap.

The boy raised his voice, shouted curses at her.

Was it Lee?

Roxie couldn't tell.

She took another step. The front door was so close. So close.

The camera suddenly felt like a thousand-pound weight against her chest. Her legs felt even heavier.

She tried to swallow, but her mouth was as dry as cotton. She was breathing shallowly, noisily.

The girl cried out again.

Roxie heard a crash. A lamp or vase shattering against the floor.

Is he going to hurt her?

The terrifying thought exploded into her mind.

Is he going to really hurt her? Is he going to kill her?

No. No way. Impossible.

Not Lee.

Not here. Not now.

I'm not going to stand here in this dark house and listen to a murder — am I? Roxie wondered, gripped with terror.

I'm not going to be a witness to a horrible murder just because of a stupid bet — am I?

"Let me go!" the girl shrieked, her voice tight with fear.

More scuffling. Another crash. The scrape of furniture against the floor.

Another slap. Another frightened, high-pitched cry.

I'm going now! Roxie told herself, staring straight at the open door. I'm going to run down the rest of the stairs, push out the door, and run to my car.

I'm going to get away from here.

I'm going to get away without being seen.

She sucked in air until her lungs were full.

Then she grabbed the camera in one hand, let go of the banister — and started to run.

Chapter 8

Roxie hurtled down the stairs.

She kept her eyes straight ahead, trained on the open front door.

Just a few more steps. A few more steps, and I'll be out of here! she told herself.

She heard the angry voices in the living room. She heard a cry of surprise.

They must have heard me, she realized.

She gripped the camera tightly in one hand and pushed herself forward.

The front door appeared to tilt and sway in front of her. But she kept her eyes on it, her destination.

Down she flew. The last step. The front entryway floor.

Three more steps to freedom. Just three more.

She had to get past the living room on the

right. And then out the front door and into the darkness of the night.

A quick glance to the living room. The lights were off. The room was as dark as the night.

Two more steps to freedom.

"Oh!" Roxie uttered a sharp cry as the flash went off. An explosion of white light revealed two startled faces in the living room.

A girl with ringlets of hair piled high on her head.

And Lee.

Was it Lee?

"Hey — !" he called.

But Roxie was out the door.

Running hard down the front lawn. Running blindly. Breathlessly. Reaching for her car keys.

The flash of white light stayed in her eyes. She saw the two startled faces in her mind as she ran. The frightened girl. The angry boy.

Lee.

Did he see her as she ran past?

Did he recognize her?

Was he coming after her?

Chapter 9

The next morning, a gray Sunday morning, humid and hot, the ringing telephone on her bed table woke Roxie.

She sat up slowly, thinking the ringing was part of a dream. The bed sheets were soaked with sweat. The long T-shirt she had slept in clung damply to her back.

She pushed a clump of brown hair back off her forehead, blinked herself awake, and reached for the phone.

"Hello?" she croaked in a sleep-fogged voice.

"Roxie? It's me. Shawna."

"Huh? Shawna? What time is it?" Roxie squinted hard at her clock radio, but her eyes refused to focus.

"Uh . . . almost nine," Shawna told her. "Did I wake you?"

"Yeah," Roxie replied. "Yuck. It's so hot in here."

Thoughts of the night before burst back into her mind. Roxie shivered, despite the heat.

She saw herself running frantically to her car, pulling out her car key with a trembling hand, flooring the gas pedal, roaring away from Lee's house without daring to look back.

Safely home, she had paced back and forth in her room for what seemed like hours.

Should she call the police? she had wondered. Was the girl in Lee's house in serious trouble?

Several times Roxie had placed her hand on the receiver, had picked it up, had started to dial — but stopped.

How do I explain what I was doing in the house? she asked herself. I can't tell the police I broke in. How do I explain how I overheard the argument?

She had returned the phone receiver to its place. It was just an argument, she tried telling herself. Nothing serious. No need to call the police.

No need to get involved.

None of my business.

Then why couldn't she get to sleep? Why

couldn't she calm down? Why did she keep reliving her desperate race to freedom again and again?

What if Lee saw me? Roxie kept asking herself, all of her muscles tight, her throat choked with fear. What if Lee recognized me? What if he knows I was hiding in his house?

So what? she argued with herself.

If Lee says anything to you, just deny it. Pretend you don't know what he's talking about. Tell Lee he's crazy. You were nowhere near his house.

Yes, Roxie decided. That was the best policy. He couldn't *prove* she was there. Besides, he probably couldn't see her in that split-second flash of light.

No way he could see her.

Repeating this to herself again and again, Roxie had finally managed to calm herself. She fell into a restless, dreamless sleep.

And now she struggled to wake up as Shawna's shrill voice rattled in her ear.

"I'm sorry to wake you," Shawna said. "But did you hear the awful news?"

"Huh? Awful news?" A cold shiver ran down Roxie's back.

"You didn't hear about Ursula?" Shawna demanded.

No — please! Roxie thought, suddenly frozen in fear. *Not Ursula! It wasn't Ursula fighting with Lee last night! Please — don't let it be Ursula!*

"Shawna — what happened to Ursula?" Roxie asked in a trembling voice.

Chapter 10

"Ursula sprained her back," Shawna reported.

Roxie opened her mouth to reply, but no sound came out. Finally, she squeaked, "She *what?*"

"Sprained her back," Shawna said.

Still feeling cold all over, Roxie let out a long sigh of relief. "How?" she asked.

"She was trying to windsurf with a bunch of kids from school. She was kind of showing off. Trying to get the sail up before everyone else. You know Ursula. She was pulling really hard and lost her footing. She fell off the board and twisted her back. We all had to help her get home."

Roxie rolled her eyes. She was wide awake now. Her heart was still racing in her chest. "And you woke me up to tell me this tragic news?" she demanded sarcastically.

"Well, I thought you'd want to know about it," Shawna replied sharply. "Ursula *is* your best friend, after all."

Roxie sighed. "Thanks, Shawna. I'll give Ursula a call and see how she's doing. Talk to you later."

Roxie hung up the phone and sat very still, waiting for her heartbeats to slow. As she pulled herself out of the damp sheets and climbed to her feet, she felt the cold dread of the night before all over again.

I'm not going to calm down, she realized. I'm not going to feel normal again until I know what happened to that girl in Lee's house.

She pulled on a sleeveless blue T-shirt and a pair of faded denim cutoffs, ran a brush quickly through her hair, and hurried to the kitchen.

"Morning." Her father, in a baggy, Hawaiian-style bathing suit, sat at the kitchen table, the Sunday newspaper spread out in front of him. He glanced up from the comics as Roxie entered.

He was slender and young-looking, a handsome man, with lively brown eyes, the same color as Roxie's, and a full head of wavy brown hair, which he brushed straight back.

"Where's Mom?" Roxie asked.

"Church," he replied through a mouthful of toast. "At least one person in this family has some decent values."

Roxie didn't reply. She picked up the front news section and quickly glanced at all the headlines. Nothing interesting.

She walked over to the coffeemaker, pulled down a mug from the cabinet, and poured herself a cup of coffee. "It's hot out already," she said softly, glancing at the heavy gray sky outside the kitchen window.

Mr. Nelson grunted in reply. Then he put down the comics and gazed at her. "You're drinking coffee? Since when do you like coffee?"

"I like it sometimes," Roxie replied, pouring in a lot of milk. She clicked on the kitchen radio and turned the dial until she found the news station.

"Please — no loud music this morning," her father begged, raising both hands in a pleading gesture. "I have two court cases I have to prepare for today. I need a little peace and quiet this morning."

"I just want to hear the news," Roxie told him, sipping the coffee.

He narrowed his eyes at her. "News? You? Have you been possessed or something?"

"You're not funny," she replied, frowning. She turned up the volume. The announcer was droning on about the weather. Possible thundershowers. Hot and humid. Then he started to read the headlines.

"Make yourself some breakfast," Mr. Nelson said, picking up the Business section. "Don't just drink coffee."

"Sshhh!" Roxie raised a finger to her lips. "I'm listening."

"Well, excuuuuuse me!" her father declared loudly. His face disappeared behind the newspaper.

"Police are heading to Hunter's Dunes where the body of a teenage girl has reportedly been found."

Roxie gasped. The white coffee mug slipped from her hand and shattered on the tile floor. Coffee puddled around her bare feet.

"Hey — !" Mr. Nelson called, startled.

"Shhh!" Roxie struggled to hear the rest of the report. But her heart was pounding too loudly. The announcer's voice rushed at her ears like thunderous ocean waves.

She could catch only disjointed words and phrases:

"Beaten . . . white, sixteen or seventeen . . .

*fully clothed . . . blond, curly hair . . . police
just arriving at the scene . . ."*

Behind her, Roxie was aware that her father
was saying something to her. But his words
were drowned out by her own horrified
thoughts.

Lee murdered her, Roxie realized.

He murdered her and dropped her body in
the dunes.

He murdered her — and I was there.

Now what?

What do I do?

Chapter 11

"Are you going to mop up the spilled coffee, or are you going to wade in it all morning?" Mr. Nelson asked, frowning.

"Oh. Sorry." Roxie shook her head hard, trying to clear her mind. She bent down to pick up the jagged pieces of broken white china.

I've got to think this out, she told herself. I've got to think very clearly.

She had a strong impulse to tell her dad everything. The whole story, from the stupid bet she'd made with Ursula, to breaking into Lee's house, to the angry fight she overheard in the dark living room.

Her father was a lawyer, after all. He would have the right advice for her. He would tell

her if she should go to the Rocky Shores police
or not.

Of *course* she should go to the police, Roxie
told herself.

But what would happen to her when she
confessed to breaking into the house?

That's not important, she argued with herself. What's important is that Lee Blume is a
murderer. He murdered that poor, frightened
girl — and I heard it.

I have to tell the police. I *have* to.

Her frantic thoughts spun through her mind,
making her dizzy. She carried a roll of paper
towels from the sink, got down on her knees,
and started to mop up the spilled coffee.

What if Lee saw me?

What if he knows it was me who ran out the
door?

I'm a witness. A *witness*!

Will he come after me next?

Who will protect me from him?

I'd better just shut up. I'd better not tell
anyone.

No. I can't keep it all inside.

She finished mopping and tossed the wet
paper towels in the trash. "Dad — ?" She
turned to face him. She pressed her back

against the kitchen counter and took a deep breath. "Dad — I have to tell you something."

He had climbed up from the table. Scratching his bare chest, he was nearly to the kitchen door. "I'm going to jog before I start on the briefs. Along the Dune Road. Want to join me?"

Roxie sighed. He hadn't heard her. "No. See you later."

He disappeared out the door. She didn't know whether to be disappointed or relieved. Glancing out the kitchen window, she could see him doing his stretching exercises.

Roxie turned away, trying to decide what to do. Her stomach gnawed at her, but she knew she couldn't eat any breakfast.

I'll go talk to Ursula, she decided. Maybe Ursula can help me figure out what to do. Besides, Ursula should know the truth about Lee.

She hurried to her room to get her sneakers. As she sat down on the bed to pull them on, she glanced at her dressertop and the flash camera caught her eye. She stared at it for a long moment.

The flash went off, Roxie remembered.

It went off as I ran past the living room.

I must have a snapshot of the two of them together.

She swallowed hard. Is it possible? she asked herself. Is it possible that I have a picture of the murder taking place?

Gripped with excitement, she tied her sneakers with shaky hands. Then she grabbed the camera and carefully rewound the film inside.

There is a one-hour developing store in town, she remembered. Is it open on Sunday? It's *got* to be!

Wrapping the yellow film roll tightly in one hand, she hurried out to her car, a dark blue Honda Civic. She placed the film carefully on the passenger seat, then started up the car.

The town of Rocky Shores, with its two rows of low white shops and restaurants, was only a ten-minute drive from Roxie's house. But this morning, the drive seemed to take hours.

She passed the white clapboard church her mother faithfully attended. The double doors had opened. People were streaming out. Roxie didn't slow down to see her mother.

She pulled the car into Main Street. The town was pretty crowded for a Sunday morning. Tourists, mostly, Roxie told herself. Not even July, and the summer crowd was already pouring in.

She glanced up at the sky. Still as dark and gray as her mood. Not much of a beach day. That's why everyone was hanging around town.

There were no parking places on the street. She had to pull into the town lot on the other side of the tiny redbrick post office.

She grabbed the film roll, slammed the car door, and hurried along the street. A crowd of people — young people, mostly — in shorts and T-shirts, were lined up outside The Cove, waiting to get into the popular little restaurant for Sunday brunch.

Roxie thought she heard someone call her name, but she didn't turn around. The one-hour developing store was in the next block, on the other side of the Book Nook, the tiny bookshop that also sold candles, soap, toys, and souvenirs.

She had to push her way past two families, talking and laughing, blocking the narrow sidewalk. A car honked. Roxie turned to see a red Pontiac with surfboards tied to the roof. She didn't recognize the teenage boys jammed inside.

She crossed the street. The small film developing shop came into view. Was it open? Roxie couldn't tell.

Gripping the film roll tightly in her hand, she picked up her pace — and nearly got run over by two girls on bikes. "Hey — get off the sidewalk!" she called to them crossly.

They ignored her and pedaled away without looking back.

Roxie made her way past the small Pic 'N' Pay market. She kept her eyes straight ahead on the film store.

Please be open. Please be open.

"Hey — Roxie!"

The familiar voice was right behind her. This time, she couldn't ignore it. She spun around, annoyed. "Oh. Hi, Terry."

"Roxie, what's up?" His eyes were wide with surprise. He hadn't brushed his red hair. It stood up on one side of his head. He was wearing a faded Ren & Stimpy T-shirt with a long rip down one side, and baggy green shorts that came down to his knees.

"Just . . . uh . . . doing some errands," Roxie told him.

"Where were you last night?" Terry demanded, brushing a blade of grass off her shoulder. "I called you. Pretty late."

"Oh. Nowhere really. Just out," Roxie replied.

That was lame! she told herself, feeling her face grow hot. *Why can't I ever be a better liar?*

"Uh . . . with my parents. Visiting some people," she added, seeing Terry's suspicious expression. "What were *you* doing?" she asked, eager to change the subject.

"Ray Metzger and I just hung out," Terry replied.

Roxie made a face. She didn't like Ray Metzger. She couldn't understand why Terry was always hanging out at Ray's house. Whenever Terry asked her to come join them, she always made an excuse not to go.

Terry gazed up at the overcast sky. "Not much of a beach day. Want to go to a movie or something later?"

"I don't know," Roxie said, biting her lower lip fretfully. "My family might have plans or something. I'm not sure."

Terry narrowed his eyes at her suspiciously. "You okay? You look kind of tense."

"No. I'm fine," she lied. "I've got to run, okay?"

"Should I call you later?" he asked.

She nodded. "Yeah. Later." Then she
turned and hurried toward the film store.

The store was open. Roxie dropped off her
film. The young woman behind the counter
told her to come back in an hour.

What should I do to kill an hour? Roxie asked
herself, stepping back out onto the crowded
street. She began to walk aimlessly, pausing
to look in shop windows.

Her stomach growled, reminding her she
had skipped breakfast. But the lines at the two
restaurants in town were too long. And everyone was in groups of two or more. She'd feel
embarrassed going in by herself.

The beach stretched three blocks from Main
Street, beyond a row of stately, old houses,
the most expensive in Rocky Shores. Roxie
thought maybe she'd go wander on the beach
for an hour until her pictures were devel-
oped.

But the sky was rapidly darkening. Storm
clouds hovered low over the storefronts. She
didn't want to be caught in the rain on the
beach.

A pink Cadillac convertible from the 1950s,
a huge boat of a car, rolled past filled with

laughing teenagers, radio music blaring into the street.

Roxie felt bitter as she watched it go by. Those kids are happy and don't have a thing on their minds except partying, she thought. They didn't witness a murder. They don't have to spend their Sunday morning waiting for a photograph of a murder to develop.

Feeling sorry for herself, she dropped down on a bench at the curb across from the post office. She slumped down and stared at her sneakers. When she raised her eyes, she saw the pay phone at the side of the post office building.

Glancing at her watch, she saw she still had twenty minutes to kill. She crossed the street and called Ursula.

Mrs. Nordquist answered, sounding rushed and frantic. Roxie asked to speak to Ursula.

"I think you'll have to call back, Roxie," Mrs. Nordquist replied. "Dr. Greene just gave Ursula some muscle relaxants. For her back. You heard about her back, right?" She didn't wait for Roxie to reply. "Well, the muscle relaxants made her very drowsy. She's half asleep and she's not making any sense at all."

"You mean — ?" Roxie started.

"She's all doped up," Mrs. Nordquist interrupted. "She sounds like she's in slow motion.
You know. At the wrong speed. I guess it'll
help her back, though."

"I could come over in a little bit," Roxie
offered.

"No. We'd better let Ursula sleep," Mrs.
Nordquist replied. "Why don't you call her tonight, Roxie? Dr. Greene says she'll be better
by then."

Roxie hung up, feeling disappointed that she
didn't get to speak to her friend. She trudged
back to the bench and waited for the hour to
be up. She tried not to think about Lee and
the frightening sounds at his house the night
before. But there was no way to force them
from her mind.

When she finally returned to the developing
store, it took the young woman a long time to
find the photo envelope. They had been filed
under the wrong name.

Roxie was practically shaking all over as she
paid the woman and took the photos. She carried them outside and leaned against the wall
to steady herself. Perspiration ran off her forehead, down her cheeks.

Do I have a snapshot of the two of them?

she wondered, pulling open the yellow-and-white outer envelope.

Do I have a snapshot of the murder?

With a trembling hand, she pulled out the glossy photos and rapidly shuffled through them.

Chapter 12

Roxie impatiently flipped past several snapshots of her parents. They had been taken at a backyard barbecue, the first of the summer at the end of May. She also hurried past some pictures of Shawna and Ursula clowning around at BladeRunners, the skating rink at the end of Seabreeze.

Her back pressed against the building, Roxie raised the photographs closer to her face as the first one of Lee's room came into view. She studied it for a brief moment, then flipped through four others. Five pictures of his room. All of them very dark. But definitely Lee's room. She recognized the cluttered bookshelves, the posters on the wall, and the model of the boat on the dresser.

And the fourth picture? The picture she had accidentally flashed of the living room?

She stared hard at it, narrowing her eyes, trying to make it come into focus, trying to figure out what exactly she had captured on film.

She shook her head and glumly lowered the stack of photos to her side as she realized she was staring at a snapshot of the ceiling light fixture.

"Oh, wow," Roxie muttered under her breath. "A stupid ceiling light. Great shot, Roxie."

A light rain started to fall as she returned to her car. She shoved the snapshots into the glove compartment, slammed it, then started up the engine.

"Now what?" she asked out loud.

She didn't feel like going home. She didn't want to think about Lee and the murdered girl — but she knew she *had* to think about it. She had to decide if she was going to tell anyone what she had heard or not.

It took a while to make her way out of town. The narrow street was backed up with cars. The rain started to come down heavier. Gray steam rose up from the pavement.

Without realizing it, Roxie headed the car out onto the Dune Road. The two-lane road curved past the rocky dunes that jutted along the sound.

She opened her window all the way. The cool raindrops felt good on her shoulder and face. On the other side of the dunes, black and purple in the eerie storm light, the waves washed steadily against the rocky shore.

The rainwater began to puddle along the side of the road. The sky grew even darker, dark enough to turn on the headlights.

What a gloomy day, Roxie thought, following the curve of the road onto the low hills she knew so well, the hills that led to the area known as Hunter's Dunes. Almost as gloomy as my mood.

She slowed the car as the headlights rolled onto a group of people clustered on the grassy dune. The twin lights played over them like spotlights.

Through the clicking windshield wipers, Roxie saw dark-uniformed police officers, paramedics in white labcoats, and several spectators in shorts and T-shirts huddled under black umbrellas.

She pulled the car to the grass and stared through the rain-spattered windshield. Up ahead stood several police cruisers, their lights flashing red, then black, red, then black, against the dark sky.

Roxie pushed open the car door and stepped out.

Red, black. Red, black.

The flashing lights held her as if in a trance. Summoned her. Pulled her to the grassy dune.

Red, black. Red, black.

She didn't notice the rain that fell steadily on her shoulders, that drenched her face. She moved forward as if in a dark, flashing dream.

Red, black. Red, black.

She joined the crowd of silent spectators. She saw their grim, tight-lipped faces. She heard low, muffled sobs.

And then her eyes fell on the dark form stretched out on the rain-soaked grass.

A bag. A black plastic bag.

Like a garbage bag, she thought. A long, slender garbage bag.

Roxie's stomach heaved as she realized she was staring down at a body bag. The girl's body bag.

She could see only sections of it. Uniformed men and women were hunched over it, studying the corpse, blocking the view.

"How long have the police been here?" she heard someone behind her murmur.

"Little more than an hour," was the whispered reply. "The rain is slowing down their work."

Roxie clapped a hand over her mouth and waited for her stomach to settle. She shut her eyes tight, but the sight of the dark, lumpy body bag, rainwater trickling off its shiny surface, refused to go away.

A sudden thought made her open her eyes. *This isn't the girl.*

The thought made Roxie's heart pound.

She brushed rainwater from her eyebrows and stepped closer, trying to get a better view. "You can't go over there," a man's low voice said from somewhere behind her.

Roxie took another step closer.

This isn't the girl.

The thought was cheering her, helping her rise above the gloomy scene on the side of the dark dune.

Why did I automatically think the murdered girl was the same girl in Lee's house? Roxie asked herself.

I jumped to a stupid conclusion.

I let my imagination run away with me.

There's no reason to think this is the same girl. It could be *any* girl.

Just because Lee was having a fight with a

girl, it doesn't mean he *killed* her! I must have been crazy, Roxie assured herself. Crazy!

Still in a trance, she stepped through the tall, wet grass. Her knees and legs were soaked with cold rainwater.

She moved up close behind the dark-uniformed police officers, huddled over the body in the bag.

"You can't go over there, miss," someone called.

Ignoring the warning, she stepped between the police officers and stared down through the falling rain.

Squinted hard. Stared through the red, then black, red, then black.

Tried to see the dead girl. Tried to see her face.

Then the body started to move, and Roxie opened her mouth in a heart-stopping scream of horror.

Chapter 13

Strong hands grabbed Roxie's shoulders. "Miss — Miss — please!" a man's voice urged.

"Did you know her?" Roxie heard a woman's hushed question. "Did you know the dead girl?"

Roxie stared straight ahead at the moving corpse. It took her a long while to realize that the body hadn't moved on its own. The police were tugging on the black plastic body bag.

"Miss — are you okay?" The hands lightened their grasp on her shoulder.

"Yes. Yes. I guess."

"Did you know her?" the woman insisted. "Do you know who she is?"

Roxie shivered and turned away. In the rain, the faces of the spectators were a dreamlike blur. They huddled under dark umbrellas, like black clouds right over their heads. They didn't blink. They stared straight ahead, stared at the black body bag collecting shiny raindrops on the grass.

Roxie took a step back. Then another. Her sneakers sank into the wet, marshy ground. Her wet hair was matted against her soaked forehead.

They were closing up the body bag. Zipping it from the bottom.

Why did I think she moved? Roxie asked herself. Why do I feel so strange, so totally, terribly strange?

And then one pale arm slid out from the top of the bag.

One pale, lifeless arm.

And as the men struggled to close the bag up in the pouring rain, the dead girl's head slid out with the arm.

And Roxie saw the girl's hair tumble out, saw the head of blond ringlets.

And started to scream again.

"Uh . . . Dad . . . sorry to bother you." Roxie poked her head in through the den door.

Mr. Nelson glanced up from the papers

spread out on the desk. "Roxie, I told you I have two different briefs to work on. Is this important?" he asked sternly.

Roxie nodded. "Yes. I think. Very."

Her father sighed and swept both hands back through his thick, brown hair. "Isn't it something you could discuss with your mother?"

Roxie couldn't keep the hurt from her face. "I really need to talk to you, Dad. Sorry if I'm taking you away from your precious briefs," she replied shrilly.

He frowned and motioned for her to sit down in the leather chair in front of the desk. Roxie walked over to the chair, but decided to stand behind it. She gripped the chairback tensely with both hands.

Mr. Nelson tossed his pen onto the pile of papers. "Well? Shoot."

Roxie cleared her throat. "Did you hear about the girl that was murdered last night? The one they found in Hunter's Dunes?"

Her father blinked. She could see he hadn't been expecting such a serious topic. "Yes," he replied quietly, staring hard into her eyes. "I ran into Ernie Cooper when I was jogging this morning. He told me about it. Did you know her?"

Roxie shook her head. She gripped the chairback tighter. "No. She didn't go to Jackson. At least I never saw her there. But . . . well . . ." She hesitated. Then she decided to plunge ahead. "I think I may know who murdered her."

"Huh?" Her father's eyes grew wide. He leaned forward over the desktop. "What are you saying?"

Roxie had figured out a way to tell her father the story without revealing that she had broken into the house. "Ursula and I know this guy," she started. "His name is Lee. Lee Blume. He moved to Rocky Shores last fall."

Mr. Nelson's eyes were riveted on Roxie. Her legs suddenly felt weak and rubbery. She stepped around to the front of the chair and sat down.

"Last night I dropped by Lee's house," she continued. "He lives on Seabreeze. I just stopped by to say hi. But the house was totally dark. And as I stepped up to the front door, I heard a girl scream."

"The front door was open?" Mr. Nelson asked.

Roxie nodded. "Yeah. It was open. I stood on the front stoop, and I heard a girl scream.

And I heard Lee. He and the girl were fighting."

Mr. Nelson scribbled a note on his pad. Then he looked up at her thoughtfully. "They were arguing? Or fighting?"

"It started out as arguing," Roxie told him. "Then I heard the girl yell, 'Let go of me!' Then I heard a crash. And she screamed. This time really frightened. Then I heard real fighting."

"And what did *you* do?" Mr. Nelson demanded, scribbling more notes on the pad. "Did you call out or try to stop them or anything?"

Roxie stared back at him. She lowered her eyes. "No. I — I ran away."

"You didn't think about calling the police?"

Roxie continued to avoid his eyes. "No. I was scared, and . . . and I didn't know if it was really a serious fight or not."

She glanced up to see her father staring at her, his eyes narrowed, his lips tight. "I suppose I should've done something," Roxie said quietly. "But I was scared. I mean — I didn't think he was going to *kill* her!"

Her voice broke. She sucked in a deep breath and held it, struggling not to burst out crying.

"Why didn't you tell me about it when you got home?" Mr. Nelson demanded softly, twirling the pen between his thumb and forefinger.

"You got home really late," Roxie replied in a quivering voice. "And I didn't know if I should bother you with it or not. I just didn't know what to do. Then when I heard this morning that they found that girl's body . . ."

Mr. Nelson climbed up slowly from the desk chair. He stepped around the desk in front of Roxie and put a gentle hand on top of her hair, the way he had always calmed her down when she was a kid. "Are you okay, Roxie?" he asked softly.

She nodded. "I guess."

"We have to go to the police," he said. "We have to go tell Chief Harms."

Roxie nodded solemnly.

They drove in silence through the rain. The steady click of the windshield wipers and the splash of the tires against the puddled road were the only sounds as Roxie slumped in the seat beside her father.

The Rocky Shores police station was a small, one-story, white clapboard building behind the post office. Two black-and-white cruisers were parked out front.

Roxie followed her father across the muddy parking lot, ducking her head from the cold rain. Mr. Nelson pushed open the wooden door and held it open for her.

They stepped into a brightly lit reception area. A police radio crackled in the background. A young officer with short, blond hair sat at a metal desk, working on a crossword puzzle.

He glanced up as Roxie and her father approached. "Hey, Nelson — how's it going?"

The Rocky Shores police all knew Roxie's father. He was the local lawyer people always called when they had any kind of legal trouble.

"I'm not sure, Farris," Mr. Nelson replied grimly. "Is Harms back there?" He gestured toward the back hall. "Roxie and I have a story for him."

"I'll check," Officer Farris said. He picked up the phone receiver, pushed a few buttons, muttered something, then nodded to Roxie's father. "Go on back. But don't get too close. He's in a bad mood and he might bite."

Roxie followed her father down the narrow hall. It opened into a row of three offices with frosted glass walls. A tall, red-faced man with wavy gray hair and bright blue eyes stepped out of the center office. "Hey, Nelson," he said. His voice was deep. He didn't smile.

"Harms, you know my daughter Roxie, right?" Mr. Nelson asked.

The police chief nodded solemnly. His blue eyes locked on Roxie. He raised a pair of silvery handcuffs in one hand.

"Roxie, I'm going to have one of my men read you your rights," he said without any emotion at all. "And I'm placing you under arrest for murder."

Chapter 14

Roxie gasped. Her breath caught in her throat.

The handcuffs dangled in front of her face.

"Harms, don't you ever get tired of that old joke?" Mr. Nelson demanded angrily.

The police chief laughed. His blue eyes twinkled. "It gets 'em every time." He smiled at Roxie. "Scared you, huh?"

Roxie managed a half-hearted smile. What a dumb joke, she thought with some bitterness. Her legs were still shaking.

"We cops have to have *some* laughs!" Chief Harms said. Then his smile faded. "It's been a rough day."

"That's why we're here," Mr. Nelson told him. "Roxie may have some information for you. About that girl's murder."

Chief Harms' lips formed an O of surprise. His eyes burned into Roxie's. "Come into my office," he said in a low voice, all seriousness now. "Both of you."

"They said they were going to pick up Lee at his house and take him to the station. To question him," Roxie said into the phone.

"Wow. I mean — wow." Shawna, on the other end of the line, sounded stunned.

A tense silence. Then Shawna said: "I knew Lee had a temper. But I never thought . . ." Her voice trailed off.

"I had to tell them the whole story three times," Roxie told her friend, tangling and untangling the phone cord around her wrist as she talked. "They asked me the same questions over and over."

The breeze through her bedroom window was cold and damp. The white curtains flapped in front of the gray evening sky. The rain had finally stopped.

"The police promised they wouldn't tell Lee that I told them about last night," Roxie continued. She felt the knot in her stomach tighten. She hadn't been able to calm down all day. Even telling the whole thing to Shawna wasn't helping. "They promised they'd leave me out of it."

"But what if Lee saw you?" Shawna asked

shrilly. "What if Lee saw you run out of his house? Then he'd know that you were the one who told the police. He'd know that you were the witness."

Roxie swallowed hard.

"He — he could come after *you* next!" Shawna stammered.

"Thanks for trying to cheer me up, Shawna," Roxie muttered dryly.

"I only meant — " Shawna started.

"The police won't let Lee go," Roxie interrupted. "He killed that girl, Shawna. He murdered her. They won't just ask him a few questions and then send him home. They'll arrest him. They'll lock him up."

"I hope so," Shawna said, sighing. "Did you tell Ursula? Have you talked to her?"

"I called her house a few minutes ago," Roxie replied, tensely wrapping the cord around her wrist. "Her mother said she was asleep. Because of the pills the doctor gave her. But I guess her back is better. She's going to work tomorrow. You know. In the office at school. I'll see her after my French class."

"Wow. Ursula will be surprised," Shawna murmured.

"Yeah," Roxie agreed. "To put it mildly. She

won't believe we made a bet to go out with a murderer."

"She won't believe she *lost* the bet!" Shawna exclaimed.

"We both lost," Roxie replied, feeling a cold chill run down her back.

"Did you really see the dead girl?" Shawna asked. "Did you get a good look at her, Roxie? What did she look like?"

"Pale," Roxie replied softly. "Very pale."

Roxie found Ursula at her desk in the school office the next morning. She was wearing a blue tank top over white tennis shorts. She had a matching blue band in her hair.

"How's the back?" Roxie asked, stepping up to the long counter.

Ursula finished typing something, then glanced up. "Much better. Still a little stiff. But I couldn't even walk yesterday."

"I called you twice," Roxie said.

"I know. Sorry I was so out of it. The muscle relaxants were unbelievable. I just conked right out."

Roxie glanced around the office. A girl and a boy she didn't recognize were typing away at keyboards on desks against the back wall.

"Can you get away?" Roxie asked, lowering her voice. "I have to talk with you."

Ursula glanced up at the wall clock. It was a little after eleven. "I guess I could take an early lunch." She opened the top desk drawer and pulled out a brown paper lunch bag. "Back in half an hour," she called to the other two workers.

They didn't even look up.

Ursula's eyes narrowed as she studied Roxie. "Why the serious face?"

"You'll see," Roxie told her. "You'll see."

They stepped out into the bright morning sunshine and followed a path behind the school building. It led them past the baseball diamonds, where a group of junior high kids were playing a noisy game of softball.

Beyond the grassy green soccer field, the path led over some low, rocky dunes to the beach. Roxie sat down on a flat rock at the edge of the beach and stared out at the blue-green water.

Although the storm clouds had disappeared, the morning air still carried a chill. Roxie could see a few sunbathers at the other end of the beach near the small boat dock. But this section was deserted.

Ursula lowered herself onto a rock across

from Roxie and pulled out a container of blue-berry yogurt from her lunch bag. As she began to slowly spoon it into her mouth, Roxie told her the whole story from the beginning.

Ursula interrupted when Roxie told her about sneaking into the side door of Lee's house to try to find his Sharks cap. "I don't believe this!" she exclaimed. "You cheater! I don't believe that Miss Straight Arrow of Rocky Shores was cheating on our bet! That's something *I* would do!"

Both girls laughed. Roxie knew that Ursula wouldn't be angry. Ursula was so competitive, she could appreciate someone else being competitive, too.

Their smiles faded and their expressions grew solemn as Roxie continued her story.

When she finished, Ursula stared at her openmouthed, the container of yogurt only half-finished in her lap. "Oh, man," Ursula murmured. "Roxie, you poor thing. You must have been so frightened."

Ursula let the yogurt container fall to the ground as she jumped to her feet. She moved quickly to Roxie and wrapped her in a comforting hug.

Roxie felt surprised by her friend's outburst of emotion. Ursula usually remained as cool and aloof as her looks. Roxie also felt grateful.

"And you don't know if Lee saw you run out or not?" Ursula asked, moving back but holding on to Roxie's shoulders.

Roxie shook her head.

"Thank goodness the police have got him!" Ursula exclaimed. She let go of Roxie and shook her head. "What a horrible story. I — I can't believe I was out on the boat with him just the day before. All alone." She shuddered.

"Shawna warned us that he had a bad temper," Roxie said quietly.

"Who was the girl?" Ursula demanded, bending to pick up the fallen yogurt container. She stuffed it back in the bag. "Did you recognize her? Who was she?"

Roxie shrugged. "Not from Rocky Shores, I'm pretty sure."

"It could've been me!" Ursula cried. And then she added, "Or you."

"I know," Roxie said, feeling the knot in her stomach tighten.

"They probably have Lee in the detention center at Rockford," Ursula said, gazing out at a sailboat tilting far on the horizon. "We'll never see him again."

Roxie wrapped her arms around her chest,

as if shielding herself. She stared out at the gleaming white sail.

Ursula glanced at her watch. "Oh, man. I'm late. I've got to run." She squeezed Roxie's hand. "You're okay, huh?"

Roxie nodded. "Yeah. I guess."

"I'll call you later." Stepping over the rocks, Ursula climbed the low dune and hurried back toward the school.

Roxie stood with her arms crossed over her chest, gazing out at the water until the sailboat faded from view. Then she lowered herself back onto the flat rock.

The bright sunlight and cool air felt soothing on her face. She watched two gulls picking at a brown clump of seaweed that had washed ashore.

Roxie could feel herself starting to relax. Ursula had been so understanding, so sympathetic. It helped to have such a good friend.

A shadow slid over her. The air suddenly felt cooler.

She turned to see what had blocked the sunlight — and stared up at Lee.

He stood above her on a jutting rock, hands at the waist of his jeans. His navy-blue T-shirt fluttered in the wind.

He glared down at her with narrowed eyes, his black hair over his forehead. The sunlight caught the small silver ring in his ear, making it glow like a diamond.

Roxie gasped.

Why wasn't he locked up? Why did the police let him go?

How long had he been standing there? Did he hear her conversation with Ursula?

Frozen on the low rock, caught in the darkness of his shadow, she watched a strange smile form slowly on his face.

"Roxie," Lee said softly, "I saw you."

Chapter 15

"I saw you," Lee repeated, stepping down beside her.

Roxie jumped to her feet.

The strange, leering smile remained on his lips, but his dark eyes were serious. Deadly serious.

A wave of panic swept over Roxie. Her eyes darted to the beach, searching for an easy escape route.

"I saw you on your way to school this morning," Lee said, bending to brush sand off the leg of his jeans. "Didn't you hear me calling you?"

He deliberately tried to scare me, Roxie thought.

He saw me at his house Saturday night. Now he's teasing me. Torturing me.

Or is he?

She eyed him warily, trying to read his expression. What thoughts were lurking behind those cold, dark eyes?

"I didn't hear you," she managed to choke out. She shoved her hands into the pockets of her tan shorts.

"You're in summer school?" he asked. He picked up a smooth, oval-shaped pebble and heaved it toward the water. It hit the ground at the shore edge and bounced into a low, blue wave.

"Yeah. French," Roxie replied uncomfortably.

Why is he here? What does he want? Why does he have that odd smile plastered on his face?

He brushed his dark hair under his cap. The smile finally faded. He picked up another smooth rock. "Is your friend in summer school, too? Ursula? Is that why she hurried away?"

So he saw us, Roxie realized, feeling a cold chill down her back. He saw us talking. Did he hear what I was saying?

Or did he know what I was telling Ursula without having to hear it?

"Ursula works," Roxie told him curtly. "I — I've got to go. I'm late."

Is he going to let me go?

Is he going to grab me now? Is he going to kill me, too?

Lee's eyes narrowed. Before Roxie could back away, he pulled his hand from his jeans pocket — and reached for her throat.

Chapter 16

"I like your locket," he said, his face expressionless.

Using two fingers, he raised the silver heart Roxie wore around her neck and studied it. "It's very delicate, isn't it?" he said, giving it a little tug, just hard enough to make Roxie uncomfortable.

He let go and raised his eyes to hers.

Roxie felt a cold chill. He's playing a cruel game, she thought.

He's deliberately trying to scare me.

And he's doing a really good job of it.

"I've got to go," she said in a tiny voice she barely recognized.

"Catch you later," Lee replied casually. He gave her a two-fingered salute, tipping his fingers against his temple.

As Roxie hurried away, running over the

rocky dune, she could feel his eyes on her, could feel the cold his shadow had lowered over her, could feel the dread of his strange, dark smile.

"So why did the police let him go?" Roxie demanded.

Mr. Nelson cleared his throat. He picked up his napkin and spread it over his lap.

"Can't we have a pleasant dinner?" Roxie's mom asked, passing the platter of chicken to Roxie. "Can't you talk about this later?"

"No. Now," Roxie insisted. She took the platter and lowered a breast and a wing onto her plate.

"Is this regular or extra-crispy?" Mr. Nelson asked.

"I got the regular," Mrs. Nelson told him, passing the container of coleslaw. "You always say the extra-crispy is too crispy. Want a biscuit?"

"Can we *please* stop talking about the chicken?" Roxie wailed.

"Your father and I have worked hard all day and we are hungry," her mother insisted.

"But I'm talking life and death here!" Roxie cried. She reached over and grabbed her father's hand, stopping it on the way to his mouth. "Why did the police let Lee go? You talked to them — right?"

Mr. Nelson set down the chicken leg. He nodded. "Lee Blume had an alibi. His parents said he was at the charity fund-raiser at the Elks' the whole evening."

"Huh? His parents said he was there?" Roxie demanded shrilly. "And the police just took their word?"

"Lots of people saw him there," Mr. Nelson replied. "The police asked a dozen people. They all said Lee was there."

"But he could have sneaked out early!" Roxie protested. "How could the police just let him go?"

"They had to," her father told her. "They had no reason to hold him."

"No reason? No reason?" Roxie shrieked. "How about he killed a girl in his living room? Isn't that a reason?"

"Roxie — please!" her mother pleaded. "You're getting all worked up."

Roxie glared across the table at her, breathing hard.

"They searched his living room, his whole house," Mr. Nelson said, picking up his chicken leg again. "They didn't see anything suspicious."

"So now you think I'm crazy?" Roxie cried in a trembling voice. "Now you think I made up the whole thing?"

Mr. Nelson raised a hand, a signal for her to lower her voice, to calm down. "I think you heard something. But you didn't see anything — right? You didn't actually see Lee Blume."

Roxie shook her head.

She couldn't admit that she had been in the house, that she had seen the girl with the blond ringlets. She had to keep to her story that she had heard the whole fight from the front stoop.

"So — what should I do?" she asked, unable to keep the fear from her voice. "What should I do now?"

"Stay away from that boy," her mother instructed, her green eyes locked on Roxie with concern.

"Don't go to the beach by yourself," Mr. Nelson added. "Be very careful, Roxie — until this whole thing is solved."

"Want to go to the beach? It's such a great night," Terry said. "How about a nice long walk?"

"Okay," Roxie told him, jumping up from

the couch. "Let me tell my parents where I'm going."

Terry had dropped by after dinner. He had seen at once that Roxie wasn't herself, that she was tense and preoccupied. "What's up?" he had asked, tapping his chubby hand on the living room couch arm.

"I'm just a little stressed out," Roxie had replied. "I don't really know why."

Of course she couldn't tell him what was really on her mind. She couldn't tell him about the bet about Lee. Terry had a temper, too.

"I keep thinking about that girl who was murdered," she confessed, lowering her eyes. "You know. The one they found at Hunter's Dunes."

"Maddy," Terry muttered.

"Huh?" Roxie gaped at him, startled. "What did you say?"

His cheeks turned bright pink. "Maddy," he repeated. "Her name was Maddy Andrews. I knew her."

"But she isn't from Rocky Shores," Roxie said, watching Terry's blush grow darker.

"Yeah. She's from Springdale," Terry replied, gazing toward the window. "I knew her at camp. Remember? That camp I was a junior counselor at two years ago?"

Roxie narrowed her eyes at him suspiciously. She didn't like the fact that he was blushing so red. "How well did you get to know her that summer, Terry?" she demanded.

Terry chuckled. "Pretty well," he replied, still avoiding her eyes.

Roxie waited for him to continue. But he stared at the window, lost in thought. Finally, he climbed to his feet and stretched his arms over his head. "How about that walk on the beach?"

The full moon was still low in the evening sky as they stepped off the dunes. Silver slips of light reflected in the choppy purple water. A million tiny pinpricks of starlight dotted the clear sky.

The scene was so beautiful, it cheered Roxie up immediately. "Piggyback ride!" she shouted, grabbing Terry's shoulders and jumping on his broad back.

He laughed and started running over the pebbly beach, neighing like a horse, bouncing her high as he ran. It was a favorite game of theirs.

Terry carried her to the shore edge, then pretended to fall into the water.

"Stop it!" she squealed.

He laughed. "Ready for a swim?"

"No! No way!" Roxie protested. "Let me off!"

Climbing down, Roxie adjusted the blue sweater she had tied around the waist of her shorts. Then she slipped off her sandals and walked barefoot along the wet, sandy shore. The cold water lapped against her ankles. The air smelled fresh and clean.

She slid her hands behind his neck and stood on tiptoe to kiss him. A long, tender kiss. His lips tasted salty. She kissed him again.

Then they walked holding hands, bumping each other gently, past other couples and groups enjoying the beach on a beautiful night.

Some kids from their school, gathered around a small campfire, their boom box blaring, called to them. Their faces were orange in the flickering light.

Roxie waved and kept walking.

Terry slipped a heavy arm around her shoulders. It felt warm and comforting.

She smiled contentedly at him. She was starting to feel better. She hadn't thought about Lee or the girl with blond ringlets for nearly an hour.

The beach curved toward a wall of black

rocks that jutted out into the water, forming a natural jetty. This part of the beach lay dark and empty. The waves were higher here. Roxie could hear them washing against the dark rock wall.

Terry bent down to pick up something from the pebbly sand. He was always finding treasures on the beach that he carried home and kept in his room. He lifted the dark, round object close to his face to examine it in the pale moonlight.

Roxie saw that it was a horseshoe crab shell. "Yuck. Put it down. It smells!" she cried, moving away from him.

Terry laughed. "Try working in a fish store all day. You won't notice bad smells at all. This smells like perfume to me!"

He tossed the shell down. They continued walking toward the rock wall. The sand gave way to large, smooth rocks. They felt hard and cold under Roxie's bare feet.

She gazed up at the full moon. Thin wisps of dark cloud floated over it, like a filmy curtain.

When she lowered her eyes, the tall white lifeguard station came into view. Roxie let out a low cry of surprise as she realized someone was sitting up there.

Not moving.

Staring.

No.

Squinting into the soft moonlight, she saw the pale bones, the gaping skull.

A skeleton.

"Whoa!" A chill of fear ran down her back.

Roxie took a hesitant step closer, trying to focus.

And staring hard, she realized it wasn't a skeleton after all. Several large, round rocks had been piled in the chair to form a human figure. Like a stony snowman.

A stone sculpture. Kids probably put it up there as a joke, Roxie realized.

What is *wrong* with me? I've *got* to calm down.

And just as she scolded herself for mistaking a pile of stones for a skeleton, she saw a dark figure moving quickly toward her over the rocks.

At first, Roxie thought she was seeing things again. Perhaps it was just a shadow cast by the clouds over the moon.

But staring straight ahead, she saw that it was a man. No. A boy. Tall and thin.

He was walking quickly, easily over the rocky ground.

Roxie stopped. He seemed to be heading straight toward her.

He came up to her quickly, looming out of the darkness.

His shadowy face hovered over hers.

"Lee!" she gasped.

His dark eyes caught the moonlight. He had that same leering smile on his face. "Roxie — what's wrong?" Lee asked in a low voice. A voice filled with unmistakable menace. "You look like a frightened rabbit."

Roxie didn't reply. She turned and searched for Terry.

"Terry?" Her voice came out a choked whisper. "Terry?"

He was gone.

Chapter 17

"What's wrong?" Lee demanded, his dark eyes burning into hers.

"I — I — you scared me," Roxie told him.

He snickered. She could see he was enjoying her fright.

She turned back, searching for Terry. Where was he? Why had he disappeared? Why had he left her alone here with this *murderer*?

"Nice night," Lee said, stepping closer, blocking her view of the water.

Roxie tried to step back, but nearly tripped over a tall, jutting rock.

"I still can't believe I can walk to the beach whenever I want," Lee continued. "Back home in Springdale, we had to drive for hours to even get to a lake!"

What does he want? Roxie asked herself,

chilled with terror. Did he follow me here? Does he plan to hurt me?

Lee took another step closer.

He was like a dark shadow, a shadow looming over her, ready to swallow her up in darkness.

"Hey — !"

Roxie turned at the sound of Terry's cry. "Terry — where'd you go?"

He lumbered out from behind a cluster of tall rocks. She saw that he was carrying something in both hands.

"Look what I found crawling around back there," he said. He was beside Roxie before he noticed Lee. "Hey, Lee — I didn't see you."

Lee gave a two-fingered salute to Terry. "What's up, Terry?"

Terry held up the treasure he had found. A large turtle, all four of its legs churning the air as Terry lifted it.

"Pretty big turtle," Lee commented, moving closer and rubbing his hand on the back of the shell. "You going to make soup?"

Terry laughed. Roxie kept her eyes warily on Lee.

"I'm going to keep him," Terry announced.

"I'm going to put him on a leash and walk him on the beach."

"Cool," Lee muttered, petting the turtle's bumpy shell.

"I'm going to name him Spot," Terry said. "Here, Spot. Here, Spot. And he'll come running when he hears his name."

"I don't think turtles run very often," Lee replied. "Except in cartoons."

"Spot loves to run — don't you, boy?" Terry asked. He raised the turtle to his face and rubbed noses with it.

"Oh, gross!" Roxie yelled, breaking her silence.

Terry laughed. "Here. I changed my mind. I'm giving the turtle to you." He shoved it toward Roxie.

Roxie stepped back, raising both hands in protest. "Me? Why me?"

"You need a pet," Terry told her, pushing the turtle into her hands. "You can keep it in that big tin pan. You know. The one you had all those snails in."

Roxie took the turtle in both hands. It was heavier than she had imagined. It immediately ducked its head and legs deep into the shell.

"See? It likes you!" Terry joked. "You going to keep it? It's an early birthday present."

"Yeah, I guess," Roxie told him. "I'll keep him for a little while, anyway. Julie, my little cousin, is supposed to come visit for a week. She'll get a kick out of him."

Roxie glanced up from the turtle and saw Lee staring at her. A hard, cold stare.

"Let's get the turtle back to your place," Terry was saying.

Lee continued to stare. "See you later," he said softly.

Lee's eyes burned meaningfully into Roxie's. "See you later," he repeated, speaking each word slowly and deliberately, a message for her alone.

A threat, she knew.

Another attempt to frighten her.

Carrying the turtle in front of her, she hurried to catch up with Terry. When she glanced back a minute later, she saw Lee still standing in the same spot, a black shadow against the rocks, staring after her.

"I put the turtle in the snail pan," Roxie told Shawna. She moved the phone closer to her on the bed.

"How big is it?" Shawna asked, yawning.

"Big," Roxie replied.

Her parents had gone to bed early. After setting up the turtle and saying good night to Terry, Roxie had wandered up to her room. Still dressed, still troubled about Lee, she didn't feel like going to sleep.

She tried reading, but couldn't concentrate. She flipped through the TV channels, but didn't find anything interesting.

Glancing at the clock radio beside her bed, she saw that it was a little after eleven. Shawna stays up late every night, Roxie remembered. So she had called Shawna.

They chatted about the turtle, about Roxie's French class, about Shawna's new boyfriend. Then Roxie decided she had to ask her about Lee.

"Did Lee ever mention a girl named Maddy when you were going with him?" Roxie asked, feeling the muscles in her neck tense as she thought about Lee.

"Maddy?" A thoughtful silence on Shawna's end. "You mean the dead girl?"

"Yeah," Roxie replied. "She was from Springdale. Same as Lee. Did he ever mention her to you?"

"No," Shawna said after another pause. "He

never talked much about Springdale. He bragged that he had a lot of girlfriends, I remember. But he never talked about them."

"You're sure?" Roxie insisted.

"Yeah. I remember Lee told me he got in some heavy-duty trouble in Springdale," Shawna continued. "I guess it was a bad time for him. He never really wanted to talk about it. I think he was happy to be making a new start here in Rocky Shores."

Some new start, Roxie thought bitterly.

"He killed her," Roxie blurted out. "I told you, Shawna. I heard the whole thing. I — "

"Are you okay?" Shawna interrupted, her voice filled with concern. "Are your parents home? Do you need me to come over or something?"

"No, I'm okay," Roxie told her, lowering her voice. "Thanks. My parents are asleep. But I'm okay. I just can't stop thinking about it, Shawna. And everywhere I go, Lee is there, staring at me, staring at me with that horrible sick smile on his face."

"He always smiles like that, Roxie," Shawna replied. "Don't pay any attention to it. I've seen that look a million times. He thinks it's sexy or something."

"I — I don't know what to do," Roxie stammered, gripping the phone so tightly, her hand ached.

"The police let him go, right?" Shawna said. "Lee was at that charity thing the night that girl was murdered. He wasn't in his house. He — "

"Wait a minute," Roxie interrupted. She removed the receiver from her ear and listened.

Yes. The sound repeated. Knocking. Downstairs.

Someone knocking on the front door.

She sat up on the bed and glanced at the clock radio. A little past eleven-thirty.

Who could be knocking this late?

Roxie knew her parents wouldn't hear it. They were such heavy sleepers.

"Shawna, I've got to hang up. Someone's downstairs."

"Call me back if you need to talk," Shawna said.

Roxie thanked her and hung up. She climbed to her feet and listened.

The knocking repeated, soft but insistent.

A burst of wind made the window curtains flap.

"Oh!" Roxie cried out, startled.

Calm down, girl, she scolded herself. You

can't jump out of your skin at every sound you hear!

Taking a slow, deep breath, she made her way down the hall to the stairs. She stopped at the landing. The lights downstairs were all turned off. The stairway was dark.

The knocking repeated. Four short knocks.

Whoever it is sure is insistent, Roxie thought.

Ignoring the heavy feeling of dread that knotted her stomach, she made her way down the dark stairway.

She jumped when a door slammed upstairs. Probably her bedroom door, she realized, her heart pounding. Probably her bedroom door pushed by the wind.

Four more knocks.

Roxie stopped at the door, raising her hand to the knob. It felt warm in her cold hand. "Who's there?" Her voice came out a hushed whisper.

No reply.

She tried again. "Who's there?" A little louder this time.

No reply.

She pressed forward and peered through the tiny, round peephole in the door.

Darkness. Only darkness.

Breathing hard, she turned the knob and pulled the door open a crack.

"Lee — what do you want?" she cried in a hoarse whisper.

Without replying, he reached out a hand to grab her.

Chapter 18

Roxie gasped and tried to slam the door shut.

But Lee had jammed his arm in the doorway.

As her eyes focused in the darkness, Roxie saw that he wasn't reaching out to grab her. He had something in his hand.

"It's yours," Lee called as she let the door swing open. "You left it on the beach."

She took it from his hand. The blue sweater she had tied around her waist.

Roxie stared at it, trying to force her heart to stop pounding.

"It's yours, right?" Lee demanded, leaning close.

The wind swayed the trees behind him. The front yard seemed to be whispering. Alive.

"Yeah. Uh . . . thanks," Roxie managed to choke out. She gripped the sweater tightly, raised it to her chest, as if for protection.

His face was covered in shadow. She couldn't see his expression.

"Thanks," Roxie repeated. "It was nice of you." She started to close the door.

He didn't move.

"My parents are asleep," Roxie told him. "So . . ."

"Want to go for a ride?" he asked suddenly.

"Huh?"

"A ride. In my boat tomorrow. After lunch, maybe?"

"No," Roxie answered quickly. Too quickly.

Even in the darkness, she could see his eyes narrow under his Sharks cap and his jaw tighten.

"I . . . I can't tomorrow," she stammered.

"Oh. Okay. Some other time," he replied in a low voice that revealed no emotion at all. Then he repeated the threat he had made on the beach: "See you later." A casual phrase — not said casually at all.

He turned and jumped down off the stoop.

She didn't watch him leave. She slammed the door shut and, breathing hard, pressed her back against it, shaking all over.

On her way to French class the next morning, Eric Frasier, a guy she barely knew, stopped her in the hallway. "Roxie, did you really see the murder?" he asked, pushing his glasses up on his nose.

Roxie gaped at him in surprise. "Who *told* you about it?" she demanded.

Eric shrugged. "It's been going around. Is it true?"

"No. It's not true," Roxie insisted angrily. "Who is talking about me, Eric?"

"Everyone," he replied. He shifted his backpack on his shoulder. "You really didn't see the murder? Ursula said — "

"Ursula?" Roxie cried shrilly, cutting him off. "Ursula's been telling everyone?"

She didn't wait for his reply. She spun around and stormed down the hall to the front office.

Why is Ursula telling everyone? Roxie asked herself. What if Terry finds out?

Maybe Lee didn't see me that night, she told herself. Maybe he doesn't know that I was there in his house.

But if everyone's talking about it, he'll hear, too. He'll find out from somebody. And then what will happen to me?

She burst into the office. Ursula and the other two workers were typing away, heads

lowered at their keyboards. They all looked
up as the door slammed behind Roxie.

"Ursula — I have to talk to you!" Roxie
blurted out in a shrill, angry voice.

Ursula's mouth opened in surprise. "Are
you okay?"

"No, I'm not! I — "

"Ssshhh!" Ursula raised a finger to her lips
and pointed to the inner office. "Not now,
Roxie," she whispered. "Mr. Rooney is here
today."

"Ursula, I don't *believe* you!" Roxie
shrieked, ignoring her friend's plea. "I —
I — "

"I'll meet you after your class," Ursula
promised, glancing worriedly at the principal's
door. "Promise. I'm only working a half-day.
I'll walk you home."

Roxie steamed all through the class. She
barely heard a word the instructor said. And
she couldn't focus on the review quiz at the
end of the hour. She was pretty sure she
flunked it.

All she could think about were kids whispering about her, telling each other how she
had been in Lee's house that night, that horrible night, the night Maddy Andrews was
murdered.

After class, Eric called to her. But she ignored his shouts and hurried to the office.

Ursula was already shutting off her computer, closing up the files she had been copying. She glanced up at Roxie and flashed her a tense smile. "TGIF," she said. "I love these half-days."

Roxie didn't say anything until they were out of the building, walking the three blocks to her house. It was a breezy, warm day, puffy clouds floating high in a pale sky. The trees shimmered overhead, showing off their fresh leaves.

"Why are you upset with me?" Ursula asked quietly, slowing her stride so that Roxie could keep up.

"Why did you tell everyone about me being in Lee's house?" Roxie demanded, unable to keep the anger out of her voice.

"Tell everyone? I didn't." Ursula stopped and turned to face Roxie. She raised her right hand, and her expression grew solmen. "I swear, Roxie. I only told a couple of people. And that was before the police let Lee go. It was when we both thought he was going to be locked up."

"How many people did you tell?" Roxie asked, frowning.

"Only one or two," Ursula said, keeping her right hand in the air as if taking an oath. "Shawna already knew. I swear, Roxie. I'm really sorry — "

"I'm sorry, too," Roxie murmured. They started walking again. Roxie felt her anger drain away. She couldn't be angry at Ursula. Ursula was her best friend.

"I haven't told Terry any of this," Roxie confessed as they crossed the street onto her block. "If he finds out — "

"You can explain it to him," Ursula assured her. "Tell him it was all my idea. Tell him it was another one of our dumb bets. He'll believe it."

"Think so?" Roxie asked doubtfully. "You know how jealous Terry can be sometimes."

"Just blame it all on me," Ursula said.

Roxie's two-story, gray-shingle house came into view. Roxie blinked when she saw the garage door was open. That's weird, she thought. My mom is always so careful to close it when she leaves in the morning.

"Know what you need?" Ursula asked suddenly, her blue eyes lighting up. "You need some fun. Something to take your mind off what happened. Want to come skating tonight?"

Roxie brushed a strand of dark hair off her forehead. "Skating?"

"Shawna and I are going to BladeRunners tonight," Ursula said. "You know. To skate. And just hang out. Why don't you come, too?"

Roxie smiled. "Sounds excellent. I'll ask Terry. Maybe he can come. He's a really good skater."

"Great," Ursula said, returning the smile.

"Come on in. I'll throw together some sandwiches for lunch," Roxie said, starting up the front walk.

She stopped when she saw the turtle on the front stoop.

How had it escaped from the tin pan?

"Hey, you — " she called to it, running to the stoop. "You have to go back where you belong."

She started to bend to pick it up — then gasped.

"Oh, Ursula — look!"

The turtle sprawled lifelessly on the concrete. Its head had been smashed flat. Its shell was cracked in a dozen places.

Roxie raised her eyes to a heavy steel mallet that lay against the front door.

"Ohh, ohhhh." Low moans escaped Roxie's throat.

Wedged under the mallet was a folded-up white sheet of paper. Roxie reached out a trembling hand and pulled up the sheet of paper. The mallet handle clanged dully against the concrete.

"What is it? What does it say?" Ursula demanded impatiently.

It took Roxie a while to unfold the paper. Then she stared at it, waiting for her eyes to focus on the crudely scribbled words.

They were written in brown crayon, printed in block letters to resemble a child's writing.

Swallowing hard, Roxie read the words out loud:

"THIS WILL BE YOU IF YOU KEEP TALKING."

Chapter 19

"Hey — ! How do you stop these things?"

Terry roared out of control across the enormous, flat skating rink, his arms straight out as if he were on a tightrope.

Roxie laughed as he crashed heavily into the railing against the far wall. He looks like a circus bear! she thought.

He turned back to her, grinning. "Is *that* how you stop?"

She skated over to him, gliding smoothly, and took his arm. "Stop clowning around. You know you're a good skater." She pulled him away from the railing.

They skated side by side, passing Ursula and Shawna and three other guys from school. Then Roxie demonstrated how to brake a Rol-

lerblade. "Now you try it," she instructed,
knowing he knew perfectly well how to brake.

Terry brushed back his red hair, a look of
concentration on his round face. He lowered
the brake pad to the rink surface — and toppled forward, sprawling on the concrete with
a loud *oof*!

"I like my way better," he grumbled, allow-
ing Roxie to pull him to his feet.

She laughed. "You've been watching Three
Stooges movies again, haven't you!"

Ursula and the others skated past, shouting
insults at Terry and shaking their heads. Roxie
skated after them, gliding gracefully, swinging
her right hand in rhythm with her legs.

She loved skating. It felt good to be moving
so quickly, so effortlessly. She took a shortcut
across the center of the rink and caught up
with Ursula.

"Not very crowded tonight," Ursula said,
leaning forward and picking up speed. "It's
such a hot night. I guess most people are at
the beach." She edged in front of Roxie.

Roxie quickened her stride, swinging her
arm harder, and caught up to her friend. The
bright green-and-blue walls of the rink flew by
in a blur.

"It's good to see you laughing," Ursula said. "Especially after this afternoon."

"My dad called the police," Roxie reported. "He told them about the turtle."

Ursula nodded solemnly.

They skated side by side for a short while. Ursula took long, easy strides. Roxie had to hurry to keep up.

The Rollerblades hummed over the concrete.

Ursula skated faster, glancing back at Roxie with a sly wink.

Before Roxie realized it, they were in a race. She lowered her head and struggled to pick up speed.

That's Ursula, she thought, breathing hard, catching up, passing her for just a moment before Ursula with her long legs took the lead again.

We can't just skate. No way. With Ursula, it has to be a race.

By the time they had circled the large rink twice, Ursula was way ahead. Roxie slowed down, hands on her knees, and watched Ursula's athletic stride, her blond hair flying behind her, catching the light of the bright overhead spotlights.

"You win!" Roxie called to her, laughing breathlessly. "For a change!"

She skated back to Terry, who was clowning around for some little kids, skating backwards, flailing his arms around, pretending to lose his balance.

The kids thought he was a riot.

Roxie grabbed the rail and stopped to catch her breath.

Shawna waved as she skated past. "Ursula wins again!" she cried to Roxie.

"So what else is new?" Roxie called back dryly.

She watched Terry and his stunts for a while. Then she turned her eyes to Shawna and the others, moving energetically in a steady rhythm around the rink.

This is so great, Roxie told herself happily. I actually forgot about Lee and the murder for a while.

I was forgetting what it's like to have a normal, happy life.

Smiling, she pushed away from the railing and started skating slowly toward Terry.

She braked quickly when she heard the scream.

A shrill, high-pitched scream.

Followed by a second one.

Screams of terror.

It took Roxie a while to recognize them, to realize that they were coming from Ursula.

Chapter 20

Roxie saw Terry spin away from the kids and begin skating rapidly in the direction of the screams. Her heart pounding, Roxie followed.

A crowd had already gathered around Ursula, who was sprawled on her back against the far wall, her knees bent, her blond hair down against the concrete.

"Ursula — what happened?" Roxie cried, pushing past several kids to get to her friend.

Ursula groaned and rolled her eyes. "I fell." She lowered her hands to the floor and tried to pull herself up. "Ow! My ankle!"

"How?" Terry asked.

"Back spasm," Ursula said. "My back gave out. I guess it wasn't ready for skating. I fell and landed on my ankle. Wow. It's swelling up already." She reached down and touched the ankle tenderly. "I don't know which hurts the most — my ankle or my back."

"Is the ankle broken?" Roxie demanded, bending over her friend with concern.

"I — I don't think so. I don't know," Ursula replied, her face pale under the bright lights. She winced in pain, but grabbed the rail and struggled to her feet.

"You've got to put ice on it right away," Shawna advised from behind Roxie.

Ursula tried to take a step, but cried out in pain. She grabbed on to Terry to keep from falling again. "Ow. Ow. Ow."

Roxie knew it really must hurt for Ursula to make such a fuss. "Let me help get the skates off," she offered, dropping to her knees and starting to unlace the right skate.

A short while later, Roxie had them both off. Ursula, still leaning on Terry, tried to walk again. But the ankle was too painful.

"I'm going to drive her home," Terry told Roxie. "Is that okay?"

Roxie nodded. "Of course."

"Then should I come back?" Terry asked.

Roxie glanced up at the wall clock over the front entrance. "It's pretty late," she told Terry. "I think I'm going to skate for a few more minutes, just to unwind. Then I'll walk home."

Terry started to protest. But Roxie reminded him it was only a ten-minute walk.

"I'll go with you," Shawna told Terry.

Roxie watched the three of them make their way to the door. Ursula leaned heavily on Terry. Shawna ran to return the Rollerblades.

With a sigh, Roxie turned back to the rink and started to skate. I just need to *move*, she thought. She loved the rush of air through her dark hair as she skated. Loved the easy feel of gliding, gliding, gliding.

The skates hummed and whirred beneath her.

She lost all track of time. She was in an easy, gliding, humming world of her own.

When she finally turned in the skates, the rink was nearly empty. Wiping perspiration from her forehead with a tissue, Roxie stepped out into the cool night.

She took a deep breath, then another. She could smell the ocean sound in the air, the sweet-sour aroma of salt and fish.

She crossed the brightly lit parking lot, empty except for two cars at the side, and made her way to the dark sidewalk. Her leg muscles tingled pleasantly from the exercise she had given them inside the rink.

Her heart was still racing. She shivered, feeling the chill night air against her overheated body.

Crossing the street, Roxie found herself thinking about Ursula. Once again, she pictured Terry helping Ursula from the rink, Ursula wincing in pain every time she had to step down on the hurt ankle.

I'll call her as soon as I get home, Roxie thought, passing along a tall hedge, dark and solid as a wall. I hope she didn't have to go to the emergency room.

Roxie was halfway down the block before she realized she was being followed.

At first she thought the rapidly approaching footsteps were those of a dog out for a late night stroll.

But then she turned and saw a shadowy figure moving along the tall hedge toward her.

Roxie sucked in a long breath of air and picked up her pace.

The footsteps behind her quickened. Came closer. Closer.

She realized she couldn't outrun her pursuer.

She stopped. Spun around.

"Who — who is it?" she choked out.

Lee stepped out of the shadows, his dark eyes glowing beneath the Sharks cap.

"Roxie — I saw you," he murmured.

Chapter 21

"I saw you skating. I called to you," Lee said.

Roxie struggled to catch her breath. "You scared me."

"Sorry," he replied, but a grin spread over his face. "I keep doing that, don't I!"

Yes, Roxie thought bitterly. *You keep deliberately scaring me.*

"How come you scare so easily?" he demanded, stepping up closer to her.

"I have to get home," Roxie replied, ignoring his question. "I have to call Ursula. She hurt her ankle."

"I'll walk you," Lee said.

"No — please!" The words burst out shrilly.

He stared at her, his smile fading. "I'll walk you just to my house," he offered. "It's on the next block." He pointed to the street sign. They were on Seabreeze.

"Really. I — " Roxie hesitated. Her heart had leaped to her throat.

I don't want to be here with Lee, she told herself.

I don't want to be walking on this dark, empty street with him. And he knows it. He's trying to frighten me. He's trying to frighten me to death.

He murdered Maddy Andrews.

He crushed my turtle. And he's threatening me.

She shuddered.

"You cold?" he asked. "Want to borrow my sweatshirt?" He started to tug at the sleeve of his dark sweatshirt.

"No," she replied curtly. "I'm okay."

"I have a T-shirt under it. You could borrow the sweatshirt."

She was walking rapidly now, taking the longest strides she could, eager to get to his house, to get rid of him. "I'm okay," she told him.

He stayed with her stride for stride. "How come I'm always scaring you?" He repeated the question. "Do you really think I'm such a scary guy?"

I think you're a murderer, Roxie thought, ignoring the sharp pain in her side, refusing to slow her pace.

They crossed the street onto his block.

"I'm just a little stressed out these days," she replied. A lame answer. But she didn't care.

Go away, Lee, she silently pleaded. *Please — just go away!*

"You need to get out on the water," Lee said quietly, putting a hand on her shoulder. His hand was hot. It burned right through the sleeve of her T-shirt. "A long boat ride will cool you right out, Roxie."

"No thanks," she murmured.

His house loomed ahead. The porch light was on, casting a yellow cone of light over the small front stoop.

I never wanted to see this house again, Roxie thought. *Never.*

Seeing the house brought back all the horror of that night. She saw herself trapped halfway down the stairway. She heard Maddy Andrews's frightened cries. Heard the slaps, the shouts, the fight.

I never want to see this house. I wish this house would burn to the ground.

And Lee with it.

She turned her head, turned her gaze across the street, and walked past.

"So how about the boat ride?" Lee was saying, his soft voice breaking through Roxie's painful thoughts. "Tomorrow afternoon? I'll take you out past the point. It's really awesome."

"I don't think so," Roxie replied. She stopped and turned to him. "We've gone past your house."

"Come out for a ride," he insisted, adjusting his Sharks cap. His dark eyes peered into hers. "Say yes. You'll enjoy it."

"I can't," Roxie repeated. "Really."

Go home, Lee. Please go home.

Her eyes darted frantically around the dark street. No one around. No one.

No one to help her if he decided to grab her.

If he decided he was through torturing her, through teasing her.

If he decided to kill her the way he killed Maddy Andrews.

No one to help her. She was all alone.

"Your house. We passed your house," she said, pointing to it.

He turned. "Huh? No, we haven't."

Her mouth dropped open in confusion.

"What do you mean? That's your house." She pointed again.

He shook his head, a strange smile on his face. "That's not my house. That's my house over there." He pointed past an empty lot to the next house, a long, low, ranch-style house.

Roxie gasped out loud.

Oh, no! she thought, raising a hand to her mouth.

That night . . .

That night . . . I was in the WRONG HOUSE!

Chapter 22

"I'd invite you in to have a Coke or something," Lee said. "But my parents have company. Maybe some other time?"

Roxie stared back at him, unable to reply. Her eyes drifted over his shoulder to the dark-shingled house where she had hidden that night.

The wrong house.

Not Lee's house.

It wasn't Lee, she told herself. *It wasn't Lee in that house. It wasn't Lee who killed that girl.*

The dark trees began to whisper. The hedges appeared to tilt and sway.

Roxie grabbed hold of a mailbox to steady herself.

I'm so mixed up, she thought. So totally mixed up.

Mixed up. Messed up. I messed up.

I blamed Lee, and it wasn't even his house.

Messed up.

Mixed up . . .

"Are you okay?" Lee asked. "You look kind of weird."

"Who lives in *that* house?" Roxie asked in a trembling voice. She pointed back to the house she had broken into.

Lee shrugged. He turned to look at it with her. "I'm not sure," he said. "People aren't too friendly in this neighborhood. I mean, they never came over and introduced themselves or anything. I think their name is Metzger."

"Metzger?" Roxie couldn't keep the surprise from her voice.

"You know them?" Lee asked. "There's a guy about our age — "

"Ray Metzger?" Roxie cried shrilly. "Goes to our school?"

"Yeah. Guess so," Lee replied. "I don't really know him, but I've seen him mowing the lawn."

"Ray Metzger is Terry's best friend," Roxie said, thinking out loud. "Terry is always hanging out at Ray's. Terry spends more time there than he does at his own house. I've never been there. I don't like Ray. But — "

Roxie cut off her words with a sharp gasp.

That's why the angry voice in the living room sounded so familiar, she thought.

I heard Terry — not Lee.

I heard Terry fighting with that girl in the dark living room.

But I didn't want to believe it.

I didn't want to believe it. So I told myself it was Lee.

Had she known all along that it had been Terry? Was that why she had been so desperate for Terry not to find out that she had been hiding in the house, that she had heard the poor girl's screams?

Had she known all along that it was Terry — and refused to accept it, refused to believe it?

Until now?

"Sure you're okay?" Lee asked, his hand on her shoulder again.

Roxie nodded. "I'm just really tired." She raised her eyes to his. She suddenly felt so guilty. I turned Lee in to the police, she realized. I accused him of killing that girl — and it wasn't even his house.

"Is that offer of a boat ride still good?" she asked. The words burst from her lips before she even thought about it.

A smile slowly spread over Lee's handsome face. "Yeah. Sure."

"I'll meet you at the dock tomorrow after my French class," Roxie told him.

"Sounds good," he replied. "Want me to walk you the rest of the way home?"

"No. Thanks. I'll be okay," Roxie said. "Sorry I was vegged out tonight. See you tomorrow."

He gave her a two-fingered salute, tipping his fingers to his temple.

She called good night and hurried away. She could hear Lee jogging to the low, ranch-style house.

His house.

Not the house Roxie had been in.

Not the house where Terry had murdered Maddy Andrews.

Terry admitted to me that he knew Maddy, Roxie suddenly remembered.

But why did he kill her? Why?

Should she go to the Rocky Shores police? Should she tell them it was Terry and not Lee?

They'll just think I'm crazy, she told herself.

There's no way they'll believe me now.

I have to break up with Terry, she decided. I have to stay away from him.

He's dangerous. So dangerous.

She made her way through the dark streets and turned onto her block. Low clouds blocked the moon, making the street even darker than usual. The trees had been whispering in a soft breeze. But now the wind had stopped. The trees were silent.

All was still. Still as death.

She walked up her front lawn and stepped onto the walk.

She was a few feet from the door when a figure darted out from the shadows at the side of the house.

He grabbed her roughly and spun her around.

"Terry!" she cried. "What are you doing here?"

Chapter 23

"Terry — let go of me!" Roxie cried.

"Did you miss me?" Terry grinned at her. He let his hands slide from her shoulders.

"I'm really tired," Roxie told him. She stared at his face. He looked like a big Huck Finn. How could he be a murderer?

How?

"Where were you?" he demanded suspiciously. "I've been waiting here for hours."

"Just skating," Roxie replied curtly. She wanted to get into the house, away from him. "How's Ursula?" she asked.

"Not too bad," Terry replied, still studying her face intently. "Her father put ice on it, and the swelling started to go down. She didn't have to go to the hospital."

"It was nice of you to drive her home," Roxie murmured, gazing toward the house.

The porch light was on, but the living room was dark.

"I'm a nice guy," Terry said, grinning his boyish grin at her. His eyes lit up. "So can I come in for a while?"

"No," Roxie answered quickly, too quickly. She could see the surprise on his face. "I'm really tired, Terry," she added. "I'll talk to you tomorrow, okay?"

She started to the front door, but stopped when she felt his hand on her shoulder. He turned her around and brought his face close to kiss her. She turned her face at the last moment, and his lips brushed her cheek.

I can't stand to kiss him, Roxie thought, feeling her stomach knot in dread. I can't kiss a murderer. I can't.

"I've got to go in. Really," she said in a whisper.

His eyes narrowed suspiciously. "Were you really just skating all this time?" he asked in a cold, hard voice.

Roxie nodded. "Yeah. Of course."

"Who with?" he demanded.

"N-nobody," Roxie stammered. She had always hated it when he started acting jealous. Now it frightened her beyond words.

His eyes burned into hers. He suddenly

seemed bigger to her, stronger, more menacing.

He could break me in two, Roxie thought with a shiver.

"Good night," she choked out, and hurried to the front door.

Slipping quickly inside, she closed the door, locked it, and hooked the chain. Her heart pounding, still seeing his dark eyes glare into hers, she made her way through the darkness to her room.

Without turning on a bedroom light, she undressed and pulled on a nightshirt. Feeling chilled, she padded to the window to close it.

Staring down to the front yard, Roxie saw that she had left the porch light on. In the pale, billowing light, she saw a large figure halfway down the driveway.

Terry.

Standing in the driveway, his hands at his sides. Staring at her house.

Just standing there, staring, staring, still as a statue.

"I really think you should tell the police," Ursula said.

"I can't," Roxie told her. She was lying on her back on top of her bedspread, holding the phone between her cheek and shoulder. "I can't just go to the police and say, 'Oops, I made a little mistake. It was Terry, not Lee.' They'll tell me to go home and call a shrink. They really will."

"Well, what are you going to do?" Ursula asked. "If Terry saw you at Metzger's house that night . . ."

"I don't know what to do," Roxie admitted. "I'm really frightened, but — "

"So you're going out with Lee tonight?" Ursula interrupted. "Where are you going?"

"Just to the movies. At the mall in Rockford," Roxie told her.

"And how was the boat ride this afternoon?" Ursula asked. Roxie heard more than a little bit of envy in Ursula's voice.

"Great," she replied. "Lee always looks so serious. You know he hardly ever smiles. I was surprised that he has such a good sense of humor."

"He's cute, too," Ursula commented dryly.

"I'm going to break up with Terry," Roxie blurted out.

"When?" Ursula asked.

"I don't know. I'm just so mixed up, Ursula. But I know I can't go out with Terry again. I'm so frightened of him. I keep picturing that poor crushed turtle. And I keep thinking that could be me."

"Listen, Roxie — at least tell your father," Ursula urged. "Your father won't think you're crazy. He'll — "

"Oh — there's a horn!" Roxie cried, scrambling to her feet. "That's Lee. Got to run, Ursula. I'll call you later. Bye."

She hung up the phone, brushed her hair quickly in front of the dresser mirror, then hurried down the stairs and out the door to meet Lee.

The movie was one of those mindless California beach movies with a bunch of college nerds chasing after blonds in bikinis. Roxie was glad. She knew she couldn't concentrate on anything with a more complicated plot.

She leaned close to Lee. They were seated up close to the screen. The theater was filled with kids and teenagers. Lee smelled of cinnamon. His dark hair tumbled down from his Sharks cap. He didn't smile, but his eyes showed that he was enjoying the film.

When the movie ended, they walked out of the theater hand in hand. Lee drove her home. They talked and laughed about what a dumb movie it was. Lee confessed that he loved dumb movies. Roxie tried to list the dumbest movies she had ever seen.

As Lee pulled the car up her driveway, Roxie stared out of the passenger window. She half-expected to see Terry, waiting at the side of the house once again.

She breathed a sigh of relief when she saw he wasn't there.

I have to break up with him tomorrow, she told herself. I have to get it over with. I have to get Terry out of my life.

I can't keep on living in fear, expecting him to pop out at me everywhere I go.

She leaned over the seat and kissed Lee good night. A long, lingering kiss that led to another. As she kissed him, she pushed away his Sharks cap and ran her hand back through his wavy, dark hair.

"See you tomorrow?" she whispered, brushing her lips against his cheek.

"Yeah. Come to the dock after class," he said. "Maybe we can go fishing or something."

"Or something," she repeated. She kissed him again. She really didn't want to get out of the car. She felt so warm, so safe.

A few minutes later, she was up in her room, sitting on the bed, gazing at the clock radio, wondering if it was too late to call Ursula.

The phone rang.

"Oh, good," Roxie said out loud. Ursula must be calling me, she thought.

But when she picked up the receiver and said hello, a cold chill rolled down her back as she recognized Terry's voice.

"I saw you, Roxie," Terry uttered in a low, menacing voice. "You shouldn't have been there."

Chapter 24

After French class the next morning, Roxie dropped into the office to ask Ursula how her ankle was feeling.

"Much better," Ursula told her, tapping her fingernails against the desktop. "I can almost get my sneaker over it without screaming in agony. Listen, Roxie — "

"Terry called me last night," Roxie interrupted. "He *did* see me that night at the Metzgers' house, Ursula. He — he threatened me. He told me I shouldn't have been there."

"Roxie, you've *got* to listen to me," Ursula said urgently, raising a hand to silence her friend. "Please let me tell you this — "

"I know what you're going to say," Roxie insisted. "You're going to tell me that I have no choice, that I have to go to the police and tell them about Terry. Well, maybe I will. I don't know."

"Roxie, listen — " Ursula pleaded.

But Mr. Rooney appeared suddenly from the inner office. Smiling at Roxie, he leaned over Ursula and began telling her something about the files she was keyboarding. Ursula kept nodding as the principal gestured to the stack of manila folders piled high on the desk.

"I'll call you later!" Roxie called, and hurried out of the office.

Ursula is probably right, she decided, stepping out into the bright sunlight and heading toward her blue Honda. Maybe I will stop by the police station later. Maybe they won't laugh at me or tell me I'm crazy.

Terry did threaten me, after all.

Thinking hard, trying to decide what to do, Roxie drove to the beach. She parked at the edge of the dune near the small boat dock, locked the car, and hurried to see Lee.

It was one of those perfect summer days. The sky was a clear, bright blue without a trace of a cloud. The air was warm and soft, gentle off the water, and not humid. The water lapped softly against the wood pilings of the dock.

Roxie's eyes followed the curve of the beach

to the right. The most popular swimming area was jammed with sunbathers. Dozens of swimmers were in the water, enjoying the calm water.

The dock area was empty. Roxie saw Lee bent over the side of his yellow boat. He looked up as she called to him, her sandals thudding on the wooden dock.

"How's it going?" she called brightly.

"Not good," he replied. He bent over an open metal toolbox and shuffled through it with both hands. "I don't believe this," he muttered unhappily.

Roxie stepped beside him. "What's wrong?"

"I'm trying to tighten this," he replied, motioning to the engine mount. "Would you believe I dropped my screwdriver in the water?" He shook his head angrily. "What a klutz," he muttered.

"You want me to put on my diving suit and get it?" she joked.

He grunted in reply and shuffled through the toolbox. "No more screwdrivers. It was my only one."

"Oh, wait!" Roxie cried. "I might have one. In my car."

He glanced up at her. "You carry around a

tool kit in case someone needs a boat repaired?"

"No. My dad makes me keep all these tools in the glove compartment. In case of an emergency, he said."

Lee's face brightened a little. He climbed to his feet and adjusted the Sharks cap over his hair. "You think you might have a Phillips screwdriver?"

"Maybe," Roxie told him. She pointed to the dune. "Go check. I'm parked on the other side."

"Be right back," Lee said. She watched him run across the small dock toward the pebbly dune. He runs so gracefully, she thought. She wondered if he played any sports. She'd never asked him about it.

She turned and gazed down at the yellow boat, bobbing gently in the sparkling blue-green water. I hope Lee can fix it, she thought. It's such a perfect day to go out for a long ride.

She turned when she heard Lee calling to her. He was standing on top of the dune, shouting something.

She cupped her ear to hear better — and then realized what the problem must be. He couldn't get into the glove compartment. She had locked the car.

"Coming!" Roxie shouted. Gripping the key in the pocket of her denim cutoffs, she ran to meet him.

They walked side by side to the car. Roxie unlocked it and pulled open the passenger door. Lee bent into the car and began pulling tools out of the cluttered glove compartment.

"Do I have the right kind?" Roxie asked, peering over his shoulder.

He pulled out a large, red-handled screwdriver. "Yes! Victory!" he cried happily, waving the screwdriver so she could see it.

"Great!" Roxie exclaimed.

Then, as Lee started to shove things back into the glove compartment, a yellow envelope toppled out, and several snapshots slid onto the seat.

Lee picked them up, his dark eyes narrowing in surprise.

"Hey — pictures of my bedroom!" he cried, turning to her. "Where'd you get these?"

Roxie gasped. She stumbled back. "So it *was* your house!" she cried in breathless horror.

Lee shut his eyes and let out a disgusted groan. When he opened them again, his expression became hard and cold. "Looks like I just messed up, Roxie," he murmured. "What a shame. It was all going so well."

Her throat choked with fear, Roxie took another step back.

"I messed up. I just messed up," Lee muttered, more to himself than to her. "And now I'm going to have to kill you, too."

Chapter 25

"I tried frightening you," Lee confessed, his eyes dark and angry in the shadow of the Sharks cap. "Then I tried winning you over. You were so eager to believe it wasn't my house you were hiding in."

He shook his head sadly. "But now I messed up."

With a frightened gasp, Roxie turned and started to run along the road.

But Lee caught up with her easily.

He grabbed one wrist and pulled her arm behind her back.

"Let *go* of me!" Roxie shrieked, trying to squirm free.

Then she felt the sharp, pointed tip of the screwdriver at the back of her neck. She stopped struggling.

"No one wants to give me a break," Lee murmured, his breath hot against her neck. "No one wants to let me have a fresh start."

He jerked Roxie's arm up hard behind her, making her cry out in pain. Keeping the screwdriver pressed against her neck, he began shoving her over the dune to the dock.

Roxie was breathing hard. Her heart thudded in her chest.

Her eyes darted over the beach.

Wasn't anyone nearby? Wasn't anyone close enough to hear her if she screamed? Wasn't anyone close enough to come save her?

No.

Laughter and loud, happy voices floated from the far end of the beach where the swimmers and sunbathers crowded together.

Here at the small boat dock she could see no one.

"Move!" Lee shouted in her ear. She felt his hot breath against the back of her neck, felt the sharp point of the screwdriver, felt his hand and shoulder roughly shoving her toward the water.

"Lee — please!" she managed to cry.

"Sure, I did some bad things in Springdale," Lee uttered, not hearing her. "Won't anyone

ever let me forget? Maddy wouldn't let me
forget. Maddy followed me to make sure I
didn't forget. Now you!"

"Lee — please — let me go!" Roxie
pleaded.

"Now you!" he repeated breathlessly. "Now
you!"

With a hard shove, he pushed her off the
edge of the dock, into the boat.

Roxie fell forward, landing on her elbows
and knees. Pain shot up her entire body. "Wh-
what are you going to do?" she stammered,
gritting her teeth, trying to force away the
pain.

He stood at the edge of the dock, staring
down at her.

"I'm going to give you a chance, Roxie," he
said softly. "I'm going to give you a chance
because I like you. I really do."

"What do you mean?" she demanded.

"I'm only going to take the boat out four or
five miles before I dump you out," Lee replied
casually. "Who knows? Maybe you can swim
back."

"I can't!" Roxie cried shrilly. "I can't swim
that far, Lee! Please — "

"I'm sorry," Lee said, frowning down at her.
"I'm really sorry, Roxie. I messed up."

"Please, Lee — " Roxie pleaded in a shrill voice she didn't recognize. Her entire body convulsed in a shudder of terror. The boat bobbed beneath her.

With a low groan, she reached up, grabbing frantically for the dock. "Let me out!" she cried, trying to pull herself up.

But Lee moved quickly to block her path. "Sorry, Roxie. Sorry. Sorry," he repeated. "I'm really sorry."

Peering up at him, Roxie saw his expression suddenly change. He turned away from her. His eyes widened in surprise.

Roxie heard footsteps over the dock. Running. An angry shout.

She cried out as Terry ran into view above her. His sleeveless blue T-shirt was drenched with sweat. His red hair was matted wetly to his forehead.

"Roxie — !" he cried, breathing hard. "I ran all the way. Ursula told me — "

"Roxie and I are going for a boat ride," Lee interrupted. "See you later, Terry."

"No!" Terry protested. "No way!" He lowered his eyes to Roxie. "I *told* you you shouldn't have been there at that movie with him. I saw you there with him that night. I warned you — "

"He — he killed that girl, Terry!" Roxie cried. "Help me!"

"Don't move, Terry. We'll see you later," Lee uttered coldly, his dark eyes glaring at Terry.

Lee started to lower himself into the boat.

But Terry dove at him, wrapping his big arms around Lee's waist.

They struggled for a moment, wrestling standing up on the deck.

Then Lee broke free of Terry's grasp.

Terry lost his balance for a second, staggered back.

Roxie cried out as Lee swung his arm back — then plunged the screwdriver into Terry's throat.

Terry let out a startled groan.

A stream of bright red blood spurted up from his neck.

His hands shot up to his throat. He uttered another cry, of pain, of shock. The cry ended in a choked whisper. Then he crumpled to the dock and didn't move.

"Terry! Terry! Terry!" Roxie screamed his name again and again. She grabbed the dock piling, scrambled frantically to pull herself up.

But, Lee, still gripping the blood-stained

screwdriver, shoved her down hard with his free hand.

She stumbled back, fell to the boat floor.

And before she could regain her footing, Lee had jumped down beside her. "Let's get this over with," he muttered, starting up the motor.

Chapter 26

With a roar, the yellow boat jolted away from the dock.

Roxie lost her balance again, tumbling to the floor. Glancing back, she could see Terry's body sprawled motionless on the dock floor.

Lee bent over the controls, muttering to himself.

I've got to get out, got to help Terry, Roxie told herself.

The boat skipped over the low, dark waves.

She took a deep breath, leaned over the side — and dove in.

She plunged down heavily, gasping from the shock of the cold as the water swept over her.

Down, down.

She struggled to kick, to swim. Her sneakers felt as if they weighed a thousand pounds each!

Her heart pounding, she raised her arms, kicked furiously, and brought herself back up to the surface. Coughing and sputtering, she sucked in a mouthful of air.

I'm turned around, she realized. I've lost my sense of direction.

Searching frantically for the shore, she spun in the water. The dock came into focus, a short swim away.

Roxie took another deep breath and held it. The current was strong, pulling her away, pulling her out farther from shore.

Ducking her head into the water, she struggled against the undertow. She began swimming hard, taking big strokes, the roar of Lee's boat in her ears.

The roar growing louder.

Closer.

With a choking gasp, she glanced up — and saw the boat moving toward her — *backing* toward her.

He's going to try to pull me out, she thought, spitting out a mouthful of salty water, stroking hard against the strong, insistent current.

No. No, he isn't.

He's backing toward me.

He wants to *cut* me! He's trying to cut me with the motor blades!

The roar grew louder, deafening, thunder in her ears, paralyzing her. She gaped at the rectangle of yellow shooting closer, closer, bright as the sun.

"No!" A terrified shriek escaped her lips, and she plunged into the water as the boat roared over her.

Blinding her. The blades churning up the dark water into a thick, frothy curtain.

Just above her head. Inches above her head.

I can't see, she realized, struggling against the churning current. I can't hear.

She surfaced gasping for air, tossing her head, struggling to see.

Blinking away the salty water, she saw the boat turning, sweeping around so quickly. Backing toward her.

The churning, sharp blades spewing up a wide warning wake.

Then moving to attack.

Her body suddenly felt so heavy, so heavy.

The current pulled her, held her, held her in place.

She dove again. Into the churning, bubbling waters.

Too late.

The boat was on top of her.

The deadly blades whirred toward her head.

Chapter 27

Silence.

I'm cut, Roxie thought.

I'm cut to pieces.

I drowned.

The water rocked and swirled around her.

It swept her up, up to the billowing surface.

Sunlight.

Or was it the yellow of the boat, coming back to slice off her head?

She sucked in a deep breath.

I'm breathing, Roxie realized. I'm alive.

Sunlight shimmered on the water, surrounded her in sparkling yellow circles of light.

And then she heard the roar once again, saw the boat backing toward her at full speed.

No! she decided. No! I'm not going to let him do this!

A desperate plan flashed into her mind.

As the boat roared closer, she could see Lee bent over the controls, his dark eyes staring out at her, aiming, aiming the blades for her head.

With a burst of strength, Roxie dove to the side, through the tossing waters, out of the boat's path.

Then she quickly twisted her body, spun, reached up her arms, and grabbed the side of the boat with both hands.

Can I tip it over? she wondered.

Am I heavy enough to tip it over and spill Lee into the water?

Chapter 28

Grasping the side of the boat with both hands, she tugged.

The boat swept along, carrying her, pulling her through its frothing wake.

Her arms ached. She tugged. Struggled to pull the boat over.

It rocked, tilted at an angle.

Roxie held on. But she realized her plan was no good. She wasn't strong enough, wasn't heavy enough.

Lee glared down at her, his expression cold and hard.

He raised the screwdriver — and slammed the blade down toward her right hand.

Roxie gasped and jerked the hand away before the blade hit.

And lost her hold on the boat.

And slipped heavily down into the cold water. Sputtering and choking.

She pulled herself back to the surface, shaking her head hard, trying to toss away the salty water that blurred her vision.

The boat. Where is the boat?

Why isn't it coming back for me? she wondered.

Squinting against the bright sunlight, she found the shore.

I'm so close to the dock, she realized.

Then she saw the dark figures running over the dock.

She saw their guns. Their guns trained on the yellow boat, which was slowly floating to the dock.

As the dark figures came into focus, Roxie realized they were police officers.

Her heart pounding, she began to swim. With strong, steady strokes, she pulled herself toward the shore.

Lee had docked the boat, she saw. Two dark-uniformed officers moved quickly to grab him.

As Roxie swam closer, she saw dark uniforms bent over Terry. She saw them lift Terry in a stretcher and carry him away.

How did they know? Roxie wondered. How did they know to come here?

A few moments later, strong hands helped pull her onto the dock. "Are you okay, miss?" a blond-haired police officer asked.

Roxie nodded. "I guess so. Terry?"

"He'll be okay," the officer replied. "We got the bleeding stopped. He should be fine."

And then Roxie saw Ursula running to her, her arms outstretched. Ursula wrapped her in a tight hug. "You're okay! You're okay! I was so scared!"

"Ursula — you — ?" Roxie managed to choke out.

"I tried to warn you, back at the school office," Ursula told her. "But you ran out. You wouldn't listen to me."

"But how did you know?" Roxie demanded breathlessly, pushing her soaked hair back off her face with both hands.

"I was typing the files," Ursula told her. "I saw Ray Metzger's address. I saw that it wasn't on Seabreeze. Ray doesn't live anywhere near there. So I knew. I knew Lee had lied to you. I tried to tell you — but you hurried off to meet him."

"So you sent Terry?" Roxie asked.

"Terry came by a few seconds after you

left. Looking for you. He was so upset that he saw you out with Lee. I told him where you were. Then I had a bad feeling. I didn't want you going out on that boat with Lee. So I called the police."

"I — I was almost fish food," Roxie murmured, shaking her head. "Ursula, you — "

"I saved your life," Ursula said, grinning. "Well, don't worry about it. You'll just owe me for as long as you live."

Roxie shivered. Ursula put an arm around her shoulders and started to lead her to the car.

At the top of the dune, Ursula suddenly let go of Roxie and reached down to the pebbly ground. She picked up a blue-and-silver cap — Lee's Sharks cap. Dusting it off, she slipped it onto her head.

"Hey, Roxie, guess what?" Ursula said, grinning. "I win the bet!"

About the Author

R. L Stine is the author of more than three dozen mysteries for young people, all of which have been best-sellers. Recent Scholastic horror titles include Call Waiting, The Baby-Sitter III, The Dead Girlfriend and Halloween Night.

In addition, he is the author of the popular monthly series Goosebumps.

Bob lives in New York City with his wife, Jane, and thirteen-year-old son, Matt.

P●INT CRiME

If you like Point Horror, you'll love Point Crime!

A murder has been committed . . . Whodunnit?
Was it the teacher, the schoolgirl, or the best friend? An
exciting new series of crime novels, with tortuous plots and
lots of suspects, designed to keep the reader guessing till
the very last page.

Kiss of Death
School for Death
Peter Beere

Avenging Angel
Final Cut
Shoot the Teacher
David Belbin

Baa Baa Dead Sheep
Jill Bennett

A Dramatic Death
Margaret Bingley

Driven to Death
Anne Cassidy

Overkill
Alane Ferguson

Death Penalty
Dennis Hamley

The Smoking Gun
Malcolm Rose

Look out for:

Concrete Evidence
Malcolm Rose

The Beat:
Missing Persons
David Belbin

Break Point
David Belbin

Accidents Will Happen
Chris Westwood

Also in the *Point Horror* series

POINT SF

Encounter worlds where men and women make
hazardous voyages through space; where time travel is a
reality and the fifth dimension a possibility; where the
ultimate horror has already happened and mankind
breaks through the barrier of technology . . .

The Obernewtyn Chronicles:
Book 1: Obernewtyn
Book 2: The Farseekers
Isobelle Carmody
A new breed of humans are born into a hostile world
struggling back from the brink of apocalypse . . .

Random Factor
Jessica Palmer
Battle rages in space. War has been erased from earth and is
now controlled by an all-powerful computer – until a random
factor enters the system . . .

First Contact
Nigel Robinson
In 1992 mankind launched the search for extra-terrestial
intelligence. Two hundred years later, someone responded . . .

Virus
Molly Brown
A mysterious virus is attacking the staff of an engineering plant
. . . Who, or *what* is responsible?

Look out for:

Strange Orbit
Margaret Simpson

Scatterlings
Isobelle Carmody

Body Snatchers
Stan Nicholls

Read Point SF and enter a new dimension . . .

Point Horror Fans Beware!

*Available now from Point Horror are tales
for the midnight hour...*

THE *Point Horror* TAPES

Two Point Horror stories are terrifyingly
brought to life in a chilling dramatisation
featuring actors from The Story Circle and
with spine tingling sound effects.

Point Horror as you've never heard
it before...

HALLOWEEN NIGHT
FUNHOUSE

available now on audiotape at your
nearest bookshop.

Listen if you dare...